Dark Horse

Tyndale House Publishers, Inc. • Carol Stream, Illinois

STARLIGHT

4

Animal Rescue

Dark Horse

DANDI DALEY MACKALL

Visit Tyndale's exciting Web site at www.tyndale.com

You can contact Dandi Daley Mackall through her Web site at www.dandibooks.com

TYNDALE and Tyndale's quill logo are registered trademarks of Tyndale House Publishers, Inc.

Dark Horse

Designed by Jacqueline L. Nuñez

Edited by Stephanie Voiland

Scripture quotations are taken from the *Holy Bible*, New Living Translation, copyright © 1996, 2004, 2007 by Tyndale House Foundation. Used by permission of Tyndale House Publishers, Inc., Carol Stream, Illinois 60188. All rights reserved.

This novel is a work of fiction. Names, characters, places, and incidents either are the product of the author's imagination or are used fictitiously. Any resemblance to actual events, locales, organizations, or persons living or dead is entirely coincidental and beyond the intent of either the author or the publisher.

ISBN-13: 978-1-4143-1271-2
ISBN-10: 1-4143-1271-7

Printed in the United States of America

15   14   13   12   11   10   09
7   6   5   4   3   2

TO ALL THE WONDERFUL READERS
who love horses as much as I do and who
have written to encourage me as I've poured
myself into the Starlight and Winnie series.

AND TO KATY,
my first reader and #1 fan.
Thank you!

Acknowledgments

I have so many people to thank for the Winnie the Horse Gentler books and the Starlight Animal Rescue books. The wonderful people at Tyndale House have made a home for me and my characters for years. Thanks to Karen Watson, who first floated the idea of having me write a horse series for Tyndale, and to Ron Beers and Carla Whitacre Mayer and Ken and Mark Taylor, who always made me feel like these books are vital. Thanks to Ramona Tucker and Jan Axford and Stephanie Voiland for amazing editing and to Katara Washington Patton for her support and direction. I'm grateful to the entire Tyndale staff, like Jan Pigott and Erin Smith, who proofread and copyedit and keep me from embarrassing myself in print. And thanks to the rest of the team—people who work, play, and pray together: Cheryl Kerwin, who does so much to get these books to readers; Jackie Nuñez, book designer extraordinaire; Rachel Griffin, product manager; Talinda Iverson, print buyer; and Steve Wagner, for his never-ending support. What a team effort this has been!

ONE

Hank Coolidge
Nice, Illinois

"Come on now, girl. I could never love that red-head more than you." I stroke Starlight's sweaty neck and lean into the turn as we canter too close to the pond. I can smell pond scum and fish. "Okay. I admit Cleo's a looker. She's got spunk and spirit. But nobody's as sweet as you, Starlight. Besides, I've always been partial to Paints."

I've been riding blind for several minutes. Keeping my eyes shut isn't easy on horseback. I don't do it often. But when I need to feel connected with my blind horse, this helps. I can sink into Starlight and trust her the way she trusts me. We've both been over every inch of this pasture hundreds of times, so there aren't any surprises left in it to trip us up.

It's been over a week since I rode Starlight, and I can't remember when I've gone this long without our ride. But the redhead—a sorrel mare named Cleopatra—has taken up every minute of my after-school time. Yesterday was the first time the mare let me get close enough to brush her. Cleo's a gorgeous Danish Warmblood, over 16 hands high, with a well-set neck, perfect shoulders, a muscular back, and strong legs . . . and so touchy it's almost impossible to imagine riding her.

We rescued Cleo from a circus a few weeks ago, at the end of October, no questions asked. But I have a million questions I'd like to ask that circus trainer, starting with what they did to the horse to make her so terrified of humans.

Starlight tosses her head, and I know instantly by the tightening I feel in her back that something's wrong. I open my eyes and ease her to a trot while I search the ground around us. No snakes. Nothing unusual I can make out.

Starlight snorts and prances in place.

Then I smell it. *Smoke.*

Please let it be leaves burning. But I know it's not. My dad's a fireman. I *know* fires.

I look back across the pasture, across two fields, and there it is, a feather of smoke rising like a thundercloud. I can't see our house. But the sky is red, like a sunset all in one spot.

Starlight lunges to a gallop before I have the sense to cue her. She's heading straight for home. I hunch low on her neck, urging her to fly. My mind's spinning. Who's in the house? Is Kat there? Is she asleep? Would she smell the smoke? Hear the alarm? Is Wes inside? Dakota?

"Come on, girl," I whisper to Starlight. We're through one pasture and galloping across the second. Grass, leaves, trees, all blur by. The acrid stench is stronger now. My eyes burn.

Out of the gray fog of smoke comes a horse racing toward us. I can't see it well enough to make out its color or features. Someone's riding it. The long strides, the outstretched neck tell me the horse is Blackfire. And that means Dakota's riding him. They're flying straight at Starlight and me.

Neither of us slows as we get closer and closer to each other. Just as I'm about to pull up Starlight so we don't crash into Blackfire, Dakota pivots her horse 180 degrees. Blackfire rears, then drops and springs into a gallop beside us.

"Is everybody out of the house?" I yell over the pounding of hooves and the rush of wind. We're galloping side by side, neck and neck.

"Yes!" She shouts something else, but I can't hear it.

But she said yes. So they're out. They're safe. We can handle anything else.

". . . horses, Hank!" Dakota shouts. And again, I can't understand what she's saying.

"What?" I yell, still galloping full speed.

"Not the house!" she screams. "The barn!"

I look toward the barn, and I can see for myself now. Smoke is billowing from the barn, not the house. Flames shoot up like fingers of fire.

"The horses?" I cry. "Dakota, are the horses out?" *Three.* Three were in the barn. Maggie and Bay Boy, the two rescues we're having trouble placing. And Cleo. I should have turned them out to pasture. But I was so anxious to ride Starlight. I left them in the barn until after my ride.

"Maggie and Bay Boy are out. Popeye and I got them," Dakota shouts.

"Cleo?" I demand. My throat closes on the word. I can't breathe. "What about Cleo?"

Dakota shakes her head. "Hank . . ." She's crying. Galloping. And crying.

"What about Cleo?" I scream.

Dakota moves in so close that Blackfire bumps my leg. "Cleo's still in the barn!"

TWO

"WHOA!" I PULL HARD ON THE REINS. Starlight slides
to a halt. "Dakota! Come back here!"

It takes her a minute to get Blackfire
slowed and turned around. "Why are you stop-
ping? Didn't you hear me? Cleo's still in the
barn! We have to get–!"

I jump off Starlight and throw the reins to
Dakota. "Stay here."

"I want to help!" she cries. But she takes
the reins.

"I don't have time to argue. Do you want
Blackfire to run back into that barn?"

She doesn't answer. I can tell she hadn't thought of that. But that's what horses do in a panic, in a fire. They try to go back to their safest spot, the place where they've felt the most at home.

I shout, "No matter what, don't let either horse any closer to the barn!" I don't think my horse would try to run to her stall, but she might.

I take off running toward the barn. My heart is pounding. Smoke fills the air. It hurts to breathe.

Someone's screaming. I think it's coming from the barn. The sound is shrill. Like a cry from some other planet. It can't be coming from a horse. From Cleo.

Dad's in his fireman's gear. He looks ridiculous. One lone fireman standing in front of a blazing barn with a garden hose.

"Dad! Dad!" I yell across the yard at him, but he doesn't turn around. The fire laps up our barn, flicking flames from the roof. It crackles and sizzles.

"Hank!" Kat's standing in front of the house when I run by. She's crying. She reaches out for me, but I can't stop.

Cleo could be on fire, burning to death right now.

Out of the corner of my eye, I see Wes struggling to hold his dogs back. They're barking at the fire, at the chaos. Wes is yelling at them. Everything is loud. I didn't know fires were so loud. Dad never said they were this loud.

I don't stop running until I'm next to Dad. "Cleo . . ." My breath's gone. I cough and spit. I'm afraid I'm going to vomit.

"I know!" Dad shouts. He moves the puny hose back and forth, a squirt gun trying to put out the sun. The gentle stream of water arcs to the roof. Flames leap to it, as if grateful for the drink.

"The fire department's on its way!" Dad yells. "They'll be here any minute."

I try to see into the barn. Smoke bursts from the windows in steady puffs. I hear glass breaking. Something falls, crashes, but I can't tell where the sound's coming from.

I move for the door.

"Hank, don't!" Dad shouts.

"I have to!" I shout back.

He grabs me from behind. I struggle to get away. We both go down.

"Listen. You can't go in there." His grip is tight. The hose is free, writhing like a snake in the dirt.

I jerk my shoulders away and break Dad's grip. I scramble to my feet. But I don't try to run into the barn again. Flames are leaping across the door. They jump, then disappear, then jump again. "I can't just let her burn to death."

"This way!" Dad's got the hose again. Aiming the water spray at the window, he pushes me toward the side of the barn. "Follow me!"

We round the barn to the back, the stall side. "She's in there," he says, pointing. Smoke rushes out of the stalls, but the flames are still up front. "Dakota got the mare out. Then that poor horse ran back in. After that, we couldn't get near her. That's when Dakota took off after you. We got the others out."

My eyes are watering. Clouds of smoke, thick and gray, swarm inside the barn, making it even harder to see into the stall. But it's Cleo's stall. She's got to be there.

"Cleo!" I scream. It's hopeless. The horse didn't come to me when things were good.

She's not going to come to me in a fire. That stall is the only safe place she's known, maybe in her whole life.

I start toward the stall.

"What are you doing?" Dad yells. He's aiming the water in a steady stream on the ground in front of me. Then he moves the spray inside the stall.

The smoke clears around the water spray. And there she is. Cleo. She's backed into a corner of the stall.

"She's there, Dad! I have to try. I'll be careful."

"She won't come with you, Hank. You know that."

I do know that. Horses in a panic think the devil they *can* see is better than the devil they can't.

That's it! "I have to blindfold her!" I pull off my sweatshirt. The heat of the smoke and fire makes my skin burn. "Douse the shirt! Now!"

Dad understands and aims his hose at my sweatshirt until it's soaked through.

I take in a deep breath and head toward the stall, tying the wet sleeves together as I go. My eyes sting so bad I can hardly see to tie the sleeves. My hands are shaking. I feel the stall door with my foot, kick it, and barge in.

"Cleo, it's me." It's so hard to see. My throat burns, like I've swallowed fire. There's a stench in here. The smoke. But something else. Like burned flesh.

I press the shirt to my eyes and over my mouth, trying to breathe in something besides smoke.

Then I see Cleo. Her eyes are bugged out. Her nostrils are huge. She's dancing in place, trying to back farther into the corner.

"Easy, girl." The words, the smoke, the burning all make me cough so hard I can't stand up straight. "Easy," I try again.

She's anything but easy. She rears. Her halter jingles. I left the halter on. I was coming right back for her after my ride. *I should have*– But I can't think of that now. I have to get her out.

Dad's yelling at me from outside the stall. A steady stream of water keeps a pathway open. Something crashes at the front of the barn. The roof creaks. Fire crackles.

Cleo rears, then rears again. Backed into the corner like this, rearing is her only defense.

I time her rears—a big one, followed by two little ones. *Big. Little, little.* When her hooves land again, I make my move. I close in and slip the wet sweatshirt over her eyes. She squeals. I step to the side of her. Her forelegs strike out, but I'm out of the way. I grab the halter. "Come on."

She won't move. Her feet are planted. She pushes her rump deeper into the corner. There's a black patch on her rump. A burn. She's been burned.

"Please, Cleo!" I know better than to try to lead her straight out. She's much stronger than I am. She's going to win any tug-of-war.

"Hank! Get out!" Dad screams. He's in the doorway now.

I'm running out of time. "Keep away!" I shout at him.

I yank the halter toward me, throwing Cleo off-balance. If I can get her in motion, make her circle, she won't know where she is. I pull her into a tight circle. She stumbles with every step. I circle her twice. Then I straighten her and head for the stall door. She gathers herself. Then she lunges.

I can't hold on. The shirt falls from her face. Dad jumps out of the way.

And Cleopatra flies through the doorway.

"Yeah!" I shout. "We did it!" I run behind her to the open doorway.

Cleo stands a few feet from the barn, her tail to me. She's shaking. A horrible cry–a scream–comes from somewhere deep inside her. It racks her rib cage, shakes her belly. And turns me to ice.

The horse rears, pawing the air. Then she spins around, ears flat back.

"Get out of the way!" Dad cries.

Cleo wants back in the barn. And I'm the only thing standing between that horse and the fire. I see the whites of her eyes. She lowers her head like a fighting bull. Bares her teeth.

And charges.

THREE

"HANK! GET OUT OF THE WAY!" Dad yells. He's dousing me with water from his hose.

Only I can't get out of the way. If Cleo runs back into the barn this time, that's it. She'll be burned alive.

I explode into action. "You get! Shoo!" I wave my arms at Cleo like a madman. "Go on!" I stamp my feet. I scream. I make noises I didn't know I had in me.

Dad turns the hose on Cleo. "Yeeehaw! Move!"

Cleo slows but keeps coming.

Dad moves the hose to spray her face.

"Get!" I scream. I run at her, arms flailing. I'm whooping and jumping and stamping. The horse rears, then pivots and takes off away from the barn at a full gallop.

Dad grabs my arm and pulls me clear of the barn. Something crashes behind me. "Hank, get away! You're too close. It's going to go!"

I feel him drag me away. I hear the creaking and groaning of the barn behind me. But all I can see is beautiful Cleopatra, her tail held high as she races away, zigzagging through the pasture. I can't take my eyes off her. She doesn't slow as she nears the fence. I think she's going to run straight into it.

Then she jumps. She sails. She flies. Without missing a stride, she lands and keeps on galloping.

"You saved her, Son." Dad's arm is around my bare shoulder. It hurts like I've been sunburned. I'm hot, then cold. Dad pulls me farther away from the fire-engulfed barn. "You saved that horse's life."

Saved her for what? What kind of a life can that horse possibly have now? Cleo will never understand what I did. She'll never trust anybody. Not after this.

"They're coming! Hear that?" Dad shouts.

Then I hear the sirens.

"Hank?" He points to the road. He slips out of his fire jacket, takes off his flannel shirt underneath, and holds it out to me. When I don't take it, he puts it on me himself.

Four fire trucks are speeding down our dirt road. They're barely visible in the clouds of dust they're stirring up. Sirens blare, getting louder and louder.

I feel like I'm watching the trucks on TV. And I'm thinking—as if the whole scene has nothing to do with me—*Nice has only two fire trucks. Wonder where they got the other trucks.*

But it's not television. The trucks are real. They're turning up our drive and bringing their sirens with them.

One of Wes's dogs breaks loose and races, barking, at the lead red fire truck.

Dad waves his arms like we're waiting to be rescued from a desert island. "We're here!" he cries. Like they can't see the flames. Like they can't see the black smoke covering our little piece of earth.

"Hank, that's your mother's van!"

My eyes are blurry. I have to blink several times before I can see her. She's driving close behind the last truck. I cough again, convulsing with the force of the coughs. It feels like my throat is on fire. And it's hot, so hot.

"Kat must have called my Annie at the hospital," Dad says, waving at Mom.

I can tell he wants to run and meet her van. But he's still holding that little hose on the fire. And that makes me want to laugh. The water trickles onto ashes now. How does that saying go? "It's like closing the barn door after the horse is out."

"What did you say?" Dad asks.

"Nothing." My mind is numb. My fingers tingle. I look down at my left hand, and my fingertips are black.

"I need to see my Annie," Dad says. "I should tell her what's going on."

"I think she knows, Dad." Again, I feel like laughing. It's the strangest sensation, like I'm caught between crying and laughter with no room in between. I watch the flames like we watch fireworks on the Fourth of July. Fire is beautiful. How could I not have known that?

"Still," Dad says, "I need to talk to your

mother." He glances to the end of the drive-way, where the van stops. The fire engines keep plowing up the drive, past the house, over the leaf-covered lawn to us.

Dad stares at the pitiful stream of water from the garden hose. Then he lays it down, finally seeing what I see.

It's no use.

"You're still too close to the barn, Hank." Dad grabs my arm and pulls.

I stumble backwards, unable to take my gaze off the flames.

"Will you be all right if I go to your mother?" Dad asks.

"I'm all right." My voice is calm, warm. My throat is still on fire. My stomach feels like flames are jumping back and forth inside of me.

"Just stay out of the way!" Dad shouts. He's already jogging around the barn, heading for Mom.

I hear the firemen shouting instructions at each other, but I can't see them through the bank of smoke.

I'm here alone with the fire.

And God.

Because God is everywhere. I've believed

that since I was five years old and maybe before that.

"Why did You let this happen?" I whisper. I'm talking to God, but it doesn't feel like prayer. "Why?" I say it louder. "Why couldn't You have caught that circus on fire? Or all those barns where people abuse Your creatures? Why us? Why did You let this happen to the Rescue?"

There's no answer.

I've known Jesus since I was five too. I've never doubted that He hears me when I pray.

Only I'm doubting it now.

I hear a whinny, long and loud.

Starlight.

I hear the whinny again, filled with terror.

For a second my heart leaps, and I'm ready to race into the barn again. Only then I remember. My horse is not in the barn. I move around to the side of the barn until I can see Starlight through the smoke and confusion.

Dakota hasn't stayed where I told her to, but she's still on her horse and holding mine. She's talking to a man I can't make out. Another man stands behind them, and I think he's got a camera. Behind Mom's van is a white van with *WXNJ News* on the side.

Are we news?

The firemen have closed in on the barn like locusts. Like termites. Thick streams of water crisscross over the roof. The sizzles and swooshes mix with the crackling of the fire. It's a sound and light show, only with water and fire.

"Hey! There's a kid back here!" One of the firemen I've never seen before runs up to me. "You! Get out of here!"

When I don't move—I can't move—he charges at me.

"Lou! That's Hank. Chester's boy." Mr. McCarthy jogs toward me. I've known "Mac" for as long as I can remember.

"I don't care who he is!" the other guy shouts. "Get him out of here!"

Mac puts his arm around my shoulder just like Dad did.

I wonder if they teach them that in firefighter's school. I don't think I'm thinking straight. But I have to. I'm Hank Coolidge, the logical one. I should be able to think straight. Maybe my logic got burned in the fire.

"Come on, Hank," Mac pleads. "I'm real sorry about all this. But you can't stay here.

I think we've got the fire under control. But it could spark up on us again." Mac waits for me to say something.

I have nothing to say.

"Are you okay?" he asks, squinting up at me.

I'm taller than him. I'm taller than Dad. I'm taller than everybody.

"Did you get burned?" He steps back and looks me over, up and down. "Why don't you go in the house, son? Let us take it from here."

I frown at Mac. I think he and Dad joined the volunteer fire department the same day.

"Hank, are you okay?" He gives up on an answer. "I need you to move." He's talking like a fireman now, not an old friend or neighbor. He pulls out a roll of yellow tape and steps toward the barn.

Another fireman—I know him, but I can't think of his name—takes the end of the yellow tape. Together they wind it around a tree and run it to the next tree.

And I get it. This is crime scene tape.

This is a crime scene.

FOUR

Winnie Willis
Ashland, Ohio

"WINNIE! CALVIN! OH NO! Come here. Oh my! This is terrible! I can't believe—!" Claire Coolidge, Catman's mother, yells out the window at us.

Catman and I have just ridden double up to the house on my horse, Nickers. I've known Mrs. Coolidge for five years, and she gets excited about a lot of things. But never like this.

Without a word, Catman slides off Nickers's rump and dashes into the house. I jump off, tell my horse to stay, then run inside after Catman.

"What's wrong? Are you okay?" I ask Mrs. Coolidge.

Her hair looks like she's been in a tornado. She's wringing her hands in front of their tiny black-and-white TV, the only black-and-white television I've ever seen. Her eyes are wide and filled with tears. "That's Chester's farm," she says. "I know it is."

Catman drops cross-legged in front of the screen. "Oh, man," he mutters.

I don't think I know a single Chester. I squint at the tiny figures on the television, but I don't recognize anybody. The camera moves from a burning barn to a farmhouse, then to a girl on a black horse. Fire trucks and firemen are everywhere.

"Chester who?" I ask.

"Uncle Chester," Catman answers. His face is inches from the TV. Images on the screen are reflected on his wire-rimmed glasses. Light splashes shadows over his broad forehead and long nose. "I'll bet that's Dakota." He points to the dark-haired girl on the black horse.

And I get it. I gasp and sink to my knees next to Catman. Chester Coolidge. Dakota. This is Starlight Animal Rescue, and it's on fire.

The newsman is sticking a microphone in the girl's face. I recognize Dakota too, from the way Kat's described her in e-mails. No wonder the camera moves in for a close-up. Dakota is beautiful, with long dark hair. She reminds me of Hawk, a Native American friend of mine who used to live in Ashland.

Mrs. Coolidge is sobbing behind me. Catman turns up the volume on the TV.

Dakota's crying, but her voice is steady. "I thought I smelled smoke. And when I looked out the window, the whole barn was in flames. Popeye was asleep on the couch in front of—"

"Popeye?" the young reporter interrupts.

"I mean, Chester Coolidge. My father. My foster father. He's a fireman—"

Catman's mother gasps. "See? I knew it! I have to call Mr. Coolidge! I have to tell him his brother's whole life is going up in flames!" They've been married at least 20 years, and they still call each other Mr. and Mrs. Coolidge.

"Shhh." Catman turns the sound all the way up.

His mother shuffles to the kitchen, to the only phone in the house.

The top corner of the TV screen says,

"LIVE." Below, it says, "Horrific barn fire in rural Illinois."

Horrific barn fire.

My stomach aches reading the words. I feel dizzy. Choked up. I know what happens to horses in barn fires.

Dakota's still talking to the reporter. "I got two of the horses out and locked in the back pasture. But Cleo ran right back into the flames." Dakota finally breaks into sobs. A woman rushes up to them and shoves the interviewer away from the horse, away from Dakota. She's short and stocky, about the size of Catman's mom.

"Right on, Aunt Annie!" Catman cheers.

But the reporter isn't giving up that easily. He holds out the mike and catches Dakota pouring out her heart to Aunt Annie.

"We have to do something!" Dakota cries. "Hank ran to the barn to get Cleo out, and I don't–I don't know if he made it! I haven't seen Cleo, and I haven't seen Hank!"

FIVE

Hank Coolidge
Nice, Illinois

"WAIT! MR. McCARTHY!" My eyes are still water-ing from the smoke, and I stumble trying to catch up with him. Mac is rolling out the yel-low tape, boxing off black ash and smoldering wood. "You think somebody set this fire, don't you?" I demand.

"Hank, you can't be here," he says.

But my mind has snapped out of shock, and it won't stop racing. "That fire didn't start itself. How could it? You know Dad. He's too careful. We've done everything we could to make the barn safe, to make sure nothing like this ever happened. Dad had you guys do inspections twice a year, even though we didn't have to!"

"I know, but–"

"We don't park anything in the barn–not the truck, not lawn mowers. No oil or aerosols, no clutter. We put in the best wiring and electric we could get when we built this place. And we're not stupid! We'd never bale wet hay. None of us would let wet straw in here." My throat burns. I don't know if it's the smoke or the tears. "Somebody must have set our barn on fire!"

"Now, we can't know if–"

"Who would do that? You have to find out. They almost burned our horses alive."

"Get him out of here!" the other fireman hollers.

"You have to go," Mac pleads. "Talk to your dad. Or to Brady, the fire marshal. They know more than I do about it. Brady's handled arson cases before."

Arson. The word sinks into the pit of my stomach.

"Hank!" Mom rushes up and throws her arms around me. "You're all right! Dakota said you ran into the burning barn after that horse! You could have been killed!"

I wrap my arms around her. She's shaking. "I'm okay. We're all okay." But my mind is spinning out plots and people and possibilities. *Arson.* What if somebody had it in for my mom? She's an oncologist. What if one of her patients died and the family blames Mom instead of the cancer?

Or Dad? People whose houses burn down end up angry. I already feel more anger than I've ever felt. What if one of the victims of a fire blamed Dad for not getting there fast enough? For not doing enough to put out their fire?

Or me? Do I have enemies? Could somebody have done this because of *me*?

Mom hasn't stopped talking, muttering. I think she's even praying, thanking God for keeping us safe, for protecting the house.

I pry myself free from her. "Mom, you should be with Kat. She's really upset."

"I know. Dad's with her. She's going to be okay," Mom says, "except she can't find her cat."

"Which one?" Kat rescues as many cats at Starlight Animal Rescue as I rescue horses or

Wes rescues dogs. We must have a dozen cats on the property, and they all hang out in the barn.

"Kitten," Mom replies.

Kitten is the only cat my sister keeps as her own. And Princess, but she's sort of unofficially adopted Dakota. The others come and go when Kat finds homes for them.

A policeman, or maybe a deputy, his hat in his hands, strides toward us. "Excuse me. Do you own a large reddish horse?"

"Cleo." Bile rises in my throat and mixes with smoke and ash. I think I'm going to be sick. "What? What happened to her?"

"She jumped my patrol car, for openers," he says. "Came tearing straight at us—me and another squad car. We tried to block the road. You know, like a roadblock?"

"What happened?" I snap. "Why did you try to trap her?" As if that horse's life could get any worse.

Mom puts her hand on my arm and squeezes. It hurts, like touching a sunburn.

"We thought we ought to contain her," he says defensively. "That horse looks dangerous. Is she?"

"If you try to trap her, she will be." As

soon as I say it, I want to take it back. I don't know what the police do to dangerous horses. "Where is she now?"

"A couple miles that way." He points northeast. "We can't leave her roaming out there. There might be kids around."

I take a deep breath to get control of myself. But the air, or the smoke, catches in my lungs. I can't stop coughing.

Mom pats my back. "Hank? You need to get out of this smoke. Come to the house with me, and—"

I turn to the police officer. My eyes are watering. There's fire in my throat and chest. "Take me to the horse. Please?" I have to try to help her or at least keep them from hurting her more than I already have. Cleo must be beyond terror. Maybe I could coax her in with feed. "Let me get some oats, and I'll—" I don't finish because I don't have oats. Not anymore. Everything I had was in the barn. How are we going to feed the horses?

I can't think about that now. I have to think about Cleo. "Will you take me to her?"

"Sure. Come on." He leads me toward his squad car.

I turn back to Mom. "Tell Dakota to put Starlight and Blackfire in the south pasture with the others." It's the pasture that's farthest from the barn.

She nods. "Be careful!" She wraps her arms around herself like she's trying to keep warm, like it's not a thousand degrees out here, like the whole world isn't on fire.

The police officer opens the back door of his squad car and motions for me to climb in. I do, wondering if this is what it feels like to be arrested. I imagine grabbing the person who started this fire and shoving *him* into the back of this car, sending him on his way to prison. That's where he belongs.

The policeman gets behind the wheel and starts the car. Then he turns to me. "I'm Deputy Hendren."

"Hank," I return.

"I figured. Sorry about you riding in back and all. Regulations."

"It's okay. I don't care. I just want to get to the horse."

He nods, and we back away from the barn.

I try not to look at it, but I can't help myself. The flames have all but died out now, leaving a sickly wash of smoldering black and gray. I turn away.

We bounce over the lawn, skirting the driveway, the fire trucks, the news van. We pass Dakota and the horses, but I don't think she notices me in the car.

Once out on the road, Deputy Hendren steps on it, and we're flying. Dust rises to the windows.

We don't talk. I want to ask him if there have been other fires around here, if he has any idea who could have set our barn on fire. But there's a screen between me and the front seat, and I can't bring myself to shout through it.

I know we've driven more than two miles when we come to a squad car parked on the shoulder of County Road 175. We slow down, but two cops wave us on, motioning us around the corner. We take the turn, and I see more squad cars, three of them. My heart's pounding. Why so many cars? Cleo's only one horse.

Then I see her. She's rearing, pitted against four policemen, each with a rope hooked to her halter or looped around her neck. She rears straight up, pulling two big men off their feet.

Cleo stands on her haunches so long I'm afraid she'll fall over backwards.

"Stop the car!" I yell. I try to get out of the patrol car, but there's no door handle on the inside. My ears hurt from Cleo's squeals. The shrill cries pierce my eardrums and travel through my nerves.

I can't take it. It's worse than I thought. Cleo. The fire. Everything. Everything is worse than I thought.

SIX

DEPUTY HENDREN shuts off the engine and hops out to open my door.

I race past him to the field. Then I shout back, "Call the vet! We need to sedate her."

I run to the nightmarish scene. Cleopatra rears and tries to throw her head, but the ropes are taut.

Forcing my legs to slow to a walk, I try to gain control of myself. Horses read fear. Cleo doesn't need to add mine to hers.

I recognize Mike Mooney, Nice chief of police, standing back and watching his men struggle. I walk up to him. "Chief Mooney, that's my horse. Would you let me try to calm her?"

"I thought she'd be yours," he says. "Sorry to hear about that fire. Everybody get out okay?"

I nod. "Everybody made it out. Thanks."

He glances at Cleo. She's pawing the ground and snorting. "This horse one of your rescues?"

"Yeah," I answer. "She was in pretty bad shape when we got her. Then the fire pushed her over the edge. She stayed in the burning barn a long time. I think maybe I could calm her down if you could get people to back off." I sound so convincing. But I'm not convinced. Not at all. Cleo didn't trust me before. She's got to hate me now. Still, I can't stand seeing her yanked around like this.

Chief Mooney has been staring at Cleo the whole time I've been talking to him. He turns to me now and seems to study me. "You sure, Hank? That horse is wild and angry. You think she'll settle down for you?"

The men holding Cleo's ropes are shouting back and forth while Cleo keeps rearing and pawing.

"I don't know," I admit. "But I'd like to try."

He nods slowly, then hollers to one of the men holding the ropes, "Matt! Hank here wants to try to talk the horse down. He's the owner."

The officer nearest us shouts back, "I don't know, Chief. The kid could get hurt."

Cleo squeals and tugs at the ropes.

Chief Mooney seems to be considering everything. Then he says, "Hank, you can try. But keep your distance. And be careful. Anything happens, you're out of there, hear?"

I nod, then move closer. The four men have formed a square around Cleo. Ropes on all sides are taut. One of the men is standing directly in front of the horse, right in her blind spot, making her even more nervous.

I move in from the side. "Take it easy, Cleo. Nobody wants to hurt you."

She snorts. I can practically see fire coming from her nostrils. She's that angry. And that raw, burned patch on her rump looks worse than I thought.

I step closer and reach for the nearest rope. The others are pulling hard the whole time. I want to slack up the rope when she gives me something, anything—a look, a drop of her head, any little sign of trust. When she comes down from the rear, I can slack the pressure, tell her she's a good girl.

I recognize the guy holding the rope I want. Kevin something. We knew each other at Nice High. Kevin's not that much older than me.

"Hank," he says, "I don't have a good feeling about this, man."

"It'll be okay." I reach for the rope.

"Look out!" somebody shouts.

Kevin jerks the rope away from me.

Cleo's hooves crash down, and immediately she tries to bolt. She gets a few feet, but the policemen have her held.

"Cleo?" I call, stepping closer.

Cleo lunges in my direction but not at me. She's just struggling, trying anything to get loose.

"Careful, man!" Kevin shouts.

"Somebody get him out of here!" barks the policeman standing in front of Cleo.

Deputy Hendren jogs up to me. "Listen, the vet's on his way. Come on. Let's go back."

"Hank!" Chief Mooney shouts, as Hendren walks me away from Cleo, toward the squad car. "You know any of these farms out here? Is there somebody who'd let us put the horse in one of these pastures?"

It's getting dark, and I have to focus to figure out where we are and whose fields we're near.

"The old McCray farm's right there!" I shout, pointing across the road. To Deputy Hendren, I explain, "The McCrays went bankrupt two years ago, and the pastures have sat empty since. The fences are still up and in good shape."

"Just a minute." Hendren dashes over to Chief Mooney and says something before jogging back to me. "All set," he says. "And the vet should be here any minute. Come on. Let's get you home."

"Maybe I should stay." But even I can hear that I don't mean it. I'm ashamed to admit it, but I don't want to see what they have to do to get Cleopatra sedated and into that pasture.

I follow the deputy to his car and tell myself that it will go easier without me. To Cleo, I'm the crazy person who chased her from the barn.

I get into the squad car and don't look

39

back. Even with the windows closed, I hear Cleo squeal. But I don't look. I want to scream and drown out her cries with my own. But I don't do that, either.

I keep my gaze trained on the floor of the car and on my own boots. I wonder how many prisoners have done this exact same thing.

I smell, rather than see, when we near home. The stench sneaks through our closed car windows.

The car stops, and I look up. One fire truck still sits on the lawn. The media van is gone. There's no sign of Dakota or Blackfire or Starlight.

People are streaming in and out of the front door. Sacks of feed line the side of the house, apparently gifts from neighbors. Mrs. Kinney and Mrs. Shaney join two other women on the front porch. They've all got foil-covered dishes, like it's a funeral gathering. Kat opens the door to let them in. Light spills outside with voices and laughter from inside.

I wait for Deputy Hendren to let me out of his car. When he does, we shake hands and don't speak. I want to thank him, but I don't trust my voice.

Like a rubberneck who can't keep from gawking at a traffic accident, I turn and stare at the barn. Only there's no barn. There are no stars, as if the fire's burned them away too. Yet even in the shadows, I can see the pile of burned boards, a glimmer of the crime scene tape, and the heavy black smoke that still hovers over the remains of what used to be Starlight Animal Rescue.

SEVEN

Winnie Willis
Ashland, Ohio

"CALM DOWN, MRS. COOLIDGE. There, there." Mr. Coolidge must have said this a hundred times already, but it hasn't done much good. His wife looks even more upset now that her husband's home.

Catman and I look on, helpless, as his mom and dad cry in each other's arms. Mr. Coolidge probably drove a hundred miles an hour to get home so fast from Smart Bart's Used Cars all the way across town.

"Maybe we could try to call them again?" I suggest. So far the line's been busy.

Mrs. Coolidge grabs her husband's cell phone. She punches in numbers. From where I'm standing, I can hear the robotic voice telling her this call cannot be completed as dialed. "It's broken!" she exclaims. "Maybe the fire burned the phone lines."

"Let me, my dear." Mr. Coolidge loosens his tie, a Bugs Bunny tie, and takes the phone. He punches a number and listens. "Busy," he says. He turns to Catman. "What else did they say on the news about Starlight Animal Rescue, Calvin?" I don't think anybody calls him Calvin Coolidge except his family.

Catman squints at the TV. It's still on, but he's got it on mute. The newscasters have moved on to some movie star award event. Half a minute was all the news an Illinois barn fire was worth, I guess.

"They said nobody was hurt in the fire," I offer. "Dakota wasn't sure about one of the horses, though." Just saying it makes me have to fight off tears. I send up a prayer for that horse and for everybody at Starlight.

Catman uses the kitchen phone to try Hank's cell phone. He listens, then leaves a message. "Dude, call us when you get this, man.

We're way bummed." He hangs up. "Hank's still not answering."

Mr. Coolidge slams his phone shut. "The line's *still* busy!" he cries. He leads his wife to the couch. Then he stands in front of the television and changes channels, flipping through the few stations they get.

I want to help. I want to do something. But I don't even have a cell to try calling the house myself. Then I get an idea. "Catman," I whisper, not wanting to rouse Mrs. Coolidge since she's quit sobbing. "Let's see if their computer's on. Maybe we could get through to somebody with an e-mail."

"Solid." He races up the stairs to the den, and I follow right behind him.

I used to hate coming into this room. I still don't like it. The walls are decorated with antlers and animal heads—bears, deer, elks, moose. What's even weirder is that nobody in the Coolidge house hunts. They hate hunting and all forms of violence. Once I tried to ask them why they have stuffed dead animals in the den. Mrs. Coolidge acted puzzled and asked if I meant the leather couch or the leather chair.

We wait for the computer to warm up. Catman logs on.

"There's something from Kat," he says.

I pull over a stuffed leather footstool. "When? When did she write it?"

But he's too focused on the e-mail to answer me.

I scoot closer and read for myself.

Catman, I don't know what to do. So here I am. I would have called you, but Mom needs the phone. She tried to call you, but your line was busy. Hank's got his cell, but we haven't seen him for over an hour.

We had a fire.

I still can't quite believe it's real. It happened so fast. We're okay. Tell everybody we're okay. But the new horse Cleopatra is in bad shape. I don't think she's burned, or at least not too bad, because she took off and ran away. Hank went with the police to bring her back.

Only there's nothing to bring her back to. The Rescue is gone. The barn is burned to the ground. How can we take care of the animals without it?

And, Catman . . . Kitten is missing.

The e-mail stops there. I imagine Kat breaking down, unable to type another word. She loves that cat. Kat's rescued so many cats, but Kitten is her favorite. Ever since Kat came to live at Starlight, she's been writing Catman for advice on how to help the cats she rescues. She and Catman have been e-mail friends for a couple of years. And Catman talks about Kat like she's his sister.

"Type something!" I urge.

"Poor kid," Catman says. His left index finger is poised over the keyboard, but he doesn't type. He bites his lip, sighs, cracks his knuckles. His eyes are misty.

"See if she's still online," I suggest. I reach across Catman and click on the instant messaging icon. "She's there! IM her."

Catman: Kat, we're here, dude! Saw it on the news. Been trying to call you. Blows my mind, little Kat.

KoolKat: Catman! I'm so glad you're here. It's awful, just awful. I know I should be thanking God that we're all okay. The house didn't catch fire (and I'm so grateful for that). But Kitten . . . oh, I can't stand to think of her being out there all by herself. She might be hurt.

Catman: Don't go there, little Kat. That's one smart, happening feline you got there. She's cool.

Catman: Kat, this is Winnie. I'm so sorry, honey. I wish we were there and could help you find Kitten. I elbowed Catman for the keyboard because I have to know about Cleopatra. Hank's been e-mailing me about that mare, the one he rescued from the circus. She's safe from the fire, right? She got out?

KoolKat: Hey, Winnie. Yeah. Cleo's okay. I think she got burned a little, but nobody can get near her to tell.

Catman: Where is she?

KoolKat: She's in a pasture not too far from here.

Catman: Catman here again. What's the skinny with Hank? The dude won't answer his cell.

KoolKat: He's acting weird. I've never seen him like this. Hank went with the police to get Cleopatra, but he came back without her. He wouldn't talk about it, but the deputy said the horse wouldn't let Hank anywhere near her. Two of the officers are still here, but Hank won't come out of his room.

Catman: The cops? The fuzz are still there? Why haven't they split yet?

There's no response. Catman and I wait, staring at the screen, at the blinking cursor. I'm just about to type another message to see if Kat's still online when she answers.

KoolKat: The police are still here because they're investigating the fire. They're asking questions about who hated us enough to burn down Starlight Animal Rescue.

EIGHT

Hank Coolidge
Nice, Illinois

"HANK, MAYBE WE should call it quits for a while." Dakota stretches in the computer chair and rubs the small of her back.

I'm not sure how long we've been sitting at the computer, but I don't care. "Look, you said you wanted to stay home from school and work on this with me. If you didn't mean it, you should have let me do this on my own."

"I didn't know we were going to sit in front of the computer all day and try to find people who hate us. I could have gone to school for that." She glances at the kitchen clock. "School's getting out about now. Man, I thought my high school teachers were slave drivers, but you beat them all." She stands. "How about we take a break? We could ride Blackfire and Starlight before Kat and Wes get home. I'll bet our horses could use the company."

"I don't have time for that."

"Well, let's go see Cleo. Maybe she's calmer now."

Something catches in my throat, and I feel the burning there. It makes me cough. Our house still smells like smoke. So do our clothes. So does the world.

"Look, Dakota, this is what I need to do. I have to find out who burned down our barn. I don't have time to play with the horses. But don't let me stop you. Do what you want." She's twice as fast as I am at typing. And she can find anything on the Internet, when it takes me forever. But I'll do this all by myself if I have to.

She sighs and drops back into the chair. "You win. But we're going in circles. You've got notes on barn fires in Illinois. A stack of printouts from news archives. There haven't been any suspicious fires in this whole county for six years, right?"

"That we know about," I admit.

"And even if it was arson, we'll never prove who did it." She reads from one of the sites she printed out. "About 90 percent of all arson cases go unsolved. No convictions."

"Doesn't mean they didn't know who did it," I tell her. "They couldn't prove it because all the evidence burned up. But they *knew*. I want to know."

"Okay." Dakota lifts her long hair off her neck, then lets it fall. "Fine. But you're all over the place with your whodunit suspects. Like these." She taps a pile of printouts I ran off. "Your mom's patients? Make that your mom's *dead* patients—which, quite frankly, is grossing me out."

"So? Maybe somebody blames *her*."

Dakota tilts her head at me, letting me know she doesn't buy it. "They blame her and then burn down your barn? Not very logical, Sherlock."

"Who said fires are logical?" She's making me mad, but I rein it in. I need Dakota's help, no matter how crazy she makes me. "Besides, I have other ideas."

"Like the fires your dad's fought?"

"What's wrong with that? If Dad's department took a long time getting to a fire, maybe somebody blames the fire department," I explain. "You know, we should work on getting response times on those fires."

Dakota isn't paying attention to a word I'm saying. She stares up at the ceiling. "Then we've got the places you've turned in for abusing horses."

"That's a strong lead, Dakota. Even you have to see that. Like that last trail ride place we got closed down. Those guys were pretty angry. You were there. You saw it. Tell me you don't think that guy with the red beard would love to get even with us for taking in their horses."

"Then why did they wait so long to do something about it?" Dakota asks. "We've already found homes for most of their horses. And you still think they did it?"

"I didn't say they did it. I'm just coming up with possibles. You think I like listing people who hate us?"

"Now there you go. Finally. That's what we need here," Dakota says. "We need lists."

I groan. Dakota is the queen of list making.

She's got journals all over the place, and she's always making her lists.

She starts to get up again. "Fine. If you don't want to take advantage of my list-making skills . . ."

"No." I put my hand on her head and press her back down in the chair. "No. You're right."

"Excuse me?" Dakota has the most infuriating, smug look on her face. "I'm *what*? I don't think I heard that correctly. Did you actually say I was right about something?"

I ignore her and her sarcasm. "Lists of possible suspects–people with grudges against any of us–could help the sheriff take us seriously. That fire inspector who came out this morning wouldn't even talk to me. He didn't want me anywhere near the barn."

"He's got to do his job," Dakota says. "Fire inspector, huh? Who knew this podunk county even had a fire inspector?"

Dakota's from Chicago, and every other town in Illinois is "podunk" to her. I let it go. I don't feel like getting into it with her. I've got more important things on my mind.

"Anyway, I can start listing the places

we've reported for animal abuse since I've lived here." She types four names.

I give her three more, but my mind's not working. I can picture every horrible scene at every farm, ranch, pasture, or stable where we reported animal abuse, but the names aren't coming back to me. "I'll have to check my records to get the names of the other places I reported—" I stop.

Dakota turns and gives me a sad smile. She gets it. I don't have records anymore.

"I should have kept copies on the computer," I mutter. Every record I had was in the wooden file cabinet in my barn office. They're not there now. This must be the 10th thing I've started to get, then remembered it wasn't there. It doesn't exist any longer because of the fire.

"Never mind," Dakota says. "The names will come to you."

"Yeah."

She shrinks the document she started and googles *fire investigations*. She gets 79,202 hits. "Too many," she says. She goes back to her list. "What about Popeye?"

"What?"

"Popeye," she repeats. "Your dad? You remember him–short, no hair." She opens a new document. "Does Popeye think it's arson?"

I shrug. I haven't been able to talk to Dad much since the fire. This morning he was already out with the fire inspector when I got up. I listened to the two of them talk, and it didn't take long to figure out that neither one of them sees what I do in this fire. I *know* it's arson.

Dakota stops typing and stares at me, silently demanding an answer to her question. *Does he think it's arson?*

"You know Dad," I finally answer. "He'd never believe anything bad about anybody."

"So that would be a no?" Dakota says. "He doesn't think somebody set the fire on purpose?"

"I don't know what he thinks. Besides, he's a fireman, not an inspector." I shove my chair back from the computer desk and walk to the window. It's a dreary day with a heavy gray sky. The fire inspector is still there, standing in the middle of the rubble. He's wearing his hard hat, even though there's nothing left to fall on him. I watch as he writes something in his notebook. He squats down. Then he writes again.

"What could he be doing out there all day?" I mutter.

"The fire inspector?" Dakota asks. "Inspecting, I suppose." She joins me at the window.

We watch the man move around what used to be our barn.

"Look on the bright side," Dakota says, which is pretty funny coming from the all-time pro of looking on the dark side. "Maybe the investigator will find out who did it—if *anybody* did it. Then we can go ride our horses."

I wheel on her. "What do you mean '*if* anybody did it'?"

Dakota starts to answer, but I don't let her.

"Somebody did it. The barn didn't just burn itself."

"Well . . . they do sometimes, Hank," she says, like she's talking me off a ledge.

I shake my head. "No. I don't know about other barns. But I do know about *our* barn. It didn't go up in flames by itself."

"Think about it," she pleads. "Sometimes things happen, and there's nobody to blame. Barns burn, and it's nobody's fault."

"You're wrong! This *is* somebody's fault."

Dakota reaches for my arm, but I shake her off and storm outside. She is so wrong. This whole nightmare is somebody's fault. And if it isn't an arsonist's fault, then whose fault is it?

Whose fault is it?

NINE

MY HEART IS POUNDING as I gaze at the pile of black ash and rubble. Either the fire inspector doesn't know I'm here or he's ignoring me. How can he ignore me? It's my barn . . . *was* my barn. I want to ask him what he's found. I have a right to know.

Wes's dog trots up to me and barks twice.

I reach down and pat him until he stops barking. "I'm okay, Rex. You don't have to worry about me."

The big German shepherd wags his tail. Wes, my foster brother, rescued the dog, and now Rex is Wes's anger-meter. The dog barks when he senses Wes is getting too angry, and I know the warning's helped Wes control his anger.

This is the first time Rex has barked at me.

A horn honks. I look up to see Mom's van swerve into the driveway. Most days Wes rides the bus, but not today. Kat and Wes are both in the van. Rex abandons me and races to greet his owner.

Kat's the first one out. Usually she's the one who has to stay home from school. Her cancer is in remission, but her kidneys aren't working like they should. Mom says that's why Kat's so weak and gets sick so often. Kat looks more like a fourth grader than a seventh grader. But when she opens her mouth, out comes the wisdom of somebody twice her age. Her cat, Kitten, still hasn't shown up. I don't think any of us want to admit that the cat probably didn't make it out of the barn.

"Hank!" Kat jogs up and hugs me. It's the first smile I've seen from her since the fire. "Wait till you hear what we've come up with."

I look at the fire inspector. He doesn't even glance our way, and I know he can hear us.

"A Fur Ball!" Kat shouts. "Isn't that a great idea?"

"What?" I'm only half listening to Kat. Mom is shouting something to me, but she's too far away.

Wes stumbles toward the house, carrying Kat's book bag and his own backpack while fighting off Rex's nonstop nuzzling and tail wagging.

"A Fur Ball!" Kat repeats. "Like a dance! I called Gram Coolidge from the car, and she's going to help me. She said they raised a ton of money with their policemen's ball last year."

Mom walks up and puts her arm around Kat. "I am so proud of these kids. It was all their idea."

"What was their idea?" I can't focus. The investigator is walking out of the rubble. I can't let him leave without talking to me.

Wes and Rex come outside again. Wes drops to the ground to wrestle with his dog. "Kat came up with hers first," he says.

"But tell him *your* ideas, Wes!" Kat beams at me. "Wait till you hear what Wes is going to do."

Wes is flat on his back now, with Rex

standing over him. "Okay, Rex. You win. I give." The dog sits at attention, and Wes gets to his feet. "These are just ideas. I don't know if they're going to work or not."

"They'll work. Go on, Wes," Mom urges.

Dakota comes out of the house. "What was all the shouting about?"

"Wes and I are going to raise money for a new barn!" Kat answers. "Gram's going to help me put on a Fur Ball and invite cats and cat owners and everything. And sell tickets and take donations."

"Cool, Kat," Dakota says.

"And listen to Wes's ideas." Kat motions for Wes to talk.

"Okay. Like maybe a doggy day care thing, where people pay to have me dog-sit or walk their dogs. And we could take pictures of people with their dogs. I thought I could set up a stand in the park. Call it 'Bark in the Park.' And maybe the old people at Nice Manor could help. Buddy already called and asked what they could do. They've got great stories about dogs they had when they were kids. So maybe we could have some kind of story night there, like 'Tales of Tails,' you know, like dog tails. Or maybe that one's stupid."

"They're wonderful ideas!" Mom exclaims. "I can't believe you came up with so many ideas so fast. We'll have that barn rebuilt in no time."

I know I should say something. They're all looking to me to be excited with them. But I'm not. Not about fur balls and dog tales. I want somebody to pay. Whoever burned our barn should be the one to rebuild it or at least pay for it.

"All I could come up with," Mom says, and I can tell she's trying to get us out the awkward moment of silence, "was elephant painting. I saw it in the paper or a magazine or something. You put paintbrushes in the trunks of elephants, and they just love to paint on canvas. Of course, we don't have any elephants."

"That's great," I say, but there's nothing behind the words, and they know it. "I mean, the cat and dog things. Thanks."

Silence falls again.

"Well," Mom says, "I don't know about the rest of you, but all this creativity is making me hungry. How about a snack?"

"No kidding," Wes says. "Think Popeye left us anything to eat?" Wes refuses to eat anything Mom fixes, and even Mom can't blame him. She can do surgery, but she can't fry an egg without burning it.

The others trail in after Mom. I feel guilty for bringing them down, but it's not in me to fake it. They're trying to help, but they're not. They just don't get it.

A stick cracks. Leaves crunch. The fire inspector is walking toward his truck.

"Wait!" I shout. "Wait a minute!"

He tosses a shovel into the back of his truck, then waits for me. He's a large man, heavier than Dad and half a foot taller. His hard hat is off, but it's left a deep hat line like a band around his head. He could be my dad's age, except for the deep wrinkles carved into his forehead.

"Did you find anything?" I ask. The stench of smoke is strong. The wind picks up leaves and black ashes, then drops them all around us like dirty snow.

He leans against his truck and pulls off his rubber boots. They're like my mud boots, the mud boots I used to have before they burned up. "My findings aren't official," he begins.

"So you did find something, then?" I knew it. I felt it. "How much longer do you have to investigate before you can give us some answers?"

"I'm finished."

"What? You're done?" I can't believe it. "I thought it would take weeks for you people to investigate."

"Well, I have to write up my report. But I don't need to come back here again," he explains.

"Then you have to tell me what you found out. How did they do it? How was the fire started?"

"Look, my findings are confidential until I turn in the report. Sorry, kid. I understand how you feel."

"No you don't. Not unless your barn burned down and your horses were scarred for life. I'm not asking you to name the arsonist or anything. I just want to know how it happened. Please?"

I think he's going to turn me down again. Then he looks out at the road, where Dad's truck is pulling in.

"That's my dad. If you can't tell me, you

can talk to him, can't you? He's a fireman. We won't tell anybody. I promise. I just have to know."

We wait in silence while Dad drives up, shuts off the engine, and walks toward us.

"Say, Brady! Didn't think you'd still be here," Dad says, like they're old friends.

"Dad, he won't tell me anything about the investigation," I complain.

"Sorry, Chester," Brady says. "You know how it is."

Dad picks up Brady's mud boots and sets them in the truck bed. "I know how it is," he admits. "But it would be nice to put this business to rest and get down to the business of rebuilding, if you know what I mean."

I hold my breath while Brady thinks this over.

"Well, I don't suppose it could hurt." He nods to the barn. "Come on. I'll show you what I found."

We follow him through what used to be our barn. I know every step of this place, even with nothing but charred boards lying everywhere. The wood over the earthen foundation has mostly burned away. Pieces of the roof lie strewn about as if someone tossed them there.

"What I look for are burn patterns," Brady begins. He's standing in the middle of what used to be our round pen. "Right away, I was pretty sure we weren't dealing with accelerants."

Dad nods. "I saw that too." He glances at me. "If somebody had dumped gasoline, there would have been a strong burn pattern."

"It was a pretty straightforward investigation," the inspector continues. "Basically I was looking for the area that was most charred. See?" He stomps the concrete footer by the old entrance. "There's no concentration anywhere there shouldn't be. Not here. Not by any of the doors."

"Ah," Dad says. He nods like he gets this.

"Wait. What does that mean?" I demand. "I don't understand what you're getting at."

Dad walks over to me. "Wherever a fire starts, you expect to find the biggest destruction at the place of origin. If it's arson, that's usually by a door, so the arsonist can escape."

"But—you said usually, right? Not always?" I feel like I'm holding on to ashes that are blowing away.

"Not always by a door," the investigator admits. "But out of place. See, in an electrical fire, the biggest burn—the most charring—will be on the wall by the electric—the wires or the fuse box."

"Was it? Was it there?" I demand. Dad and I bought the best, the safest wiring we could find. We were so careful.

"Nothing unusual there either. I ruled out faulty wiring pretty quick." Brady walks to where the loft used to be. The whole hayloft collapsed in the fire, stacking burned rafters onto burned floor. "Here's where I think it started."

Dad and I move there, not stepping on the area, like it's a grave site.

"It doesn't look worse than anywhere else to me," I insist. "Look at this." I pick up a piece of straw that hasn't burned up. It's gray from smoke, brittle, but not burned up.

"Straw smokes and smolders," Dad explains. "It doesn't always burn. Look at the floor, Hank. It's blacker than black here."

"But it can't be the loft," I insist. "Dad, tell him. We never put up wet hay. We know how combustible it is. We'd never do that."

"Not saying you did, son," the investigator says. "Sometimes something makes a hole in the roof. Water gets in. You just never know. What I do know, what I'm putting in the report, is that this fire was not caused by arson."

TEN

Winnie Willis
Ashland, Ohio

NOTHING IN THE WORLD works on me like a ride on my horse, whether I'm riding alone or riding double with Catman, like I am now. I signal Nickers, and we lunge into a canter.

Catman has to hang on, his long arms wrapping around my waist. It's been great having him back in town again. When he graduated last year, he decided to take a whole year off to make a "cat-umentary"—a documentary about the life of cats in rural America. He's traveled all over the country filming felines. "Far out!" he shouts.

The wind blows my hair and cools my skin. Nickers's hooves strike the fallen leaves with a *swish, crunch*. I feel the tension and worries blow away. I don't think I've slept since we learned about the fire. I've been too worried about Cleo and Hank, Kat and her kitten, and everybody at Starlight Animal Rescue.

But it's more than feeling helpless about the fire in Illinois. We've had our share of tension in Ohio, too. In the Willis household, money is always tight. But for the past year, we haven't had any money to be tight with. Nobody wanted to buy Madeline's last invention or Dad's last two. My little sister, Lizzy, has had to use her babysitting money to buy groceries. And I've had to go back to mucking stalls at Spidells' Stable-Mart just to keep Nickers in feed.

So far, being a senior in high school hasn't been all that great either. Already, kids are talking about where they're going after graduation, what they're going to do with the rest of their lives.

And I'm not.

I always thought I was meant to be a veterinarian because I love horses so much.

I never stopped to think how much it would cost. But when you're a senior, suddenly it's time to think about that kind of thing. It's time to get real. I couldn't even come up with the cash to apply to OSU, much less to get the equipment for their pre-vet courses. Dad would have borrowed the money, but what then? I'm not smart enough to get scholarship money. I'd never be able to afford veterinary school, even if I made it through the pre-vet program. Better to realize that now instead of later.

We canter up the long dirt drive to Catman's house. I slow Nickers to a spirited walk. I think both of us, maybe all three of us, could have kept going all day. Maybe we should have. The tension that drained from me on the ride is already creeping back.

"Calvin! Winnie!" Mrs. Coolidge steps out of the house and waves us over.

For a second I freeze, remembering the way she yelled for us to hear the awful news about the fire.

But this time she's all smiles, so I relax a little. Mrs. Coolidge motions us to the side yard, where Catman's dad is wrestling with some kind of plastic lawn ornament. I don't ask. The whole Coolidge place is pretty hard to explain. The three-story house with boarded-up windows reminds me of the spooky houses you see in scary movies. Strings of orange and red lights dangle from the roof, where they stay all year.

"What's the skinny?" Catman asks, sliding off Nickers's rump.

I dismount and unbridle Nickers so she can graze. The Coolidge yard is one of my horse's favorite places to visit because the Coolidges almost never cut their grass.

"It wasn't arson!" Mrs. Coolidge announces. "I am so very relieved. I just couldn't imagine anyone doing something so cruel as to burn down the Rescue. Mr. Coolidge just got off the phone with his brother. Tell them, dear."

We join Catman's dad on the lawn, where he's trying to get the life-size plastic Pilgrims to stand up without leaning against the Native Americans.

"The official determination according to my brother, Chester Coolidge, is that the fire is not believed to have been suspicious in origin." Bart Coolidge pats the little plastic Pilgrim boy on the head, as if he'd been the bearer of this good news.

Mrs. Coolidge dashes to the garage, where I've never seen a parked car, only plastic lawn ornaments. She comes out with a giant plastic turkey, a *green* turkey.

"Need some help?" I volunteer.

"Thank you, Winnie." She staggers slightly and shifts the turkey from under her arm to directly in front of her. Between her and us sits a row of plastic jack-o'-lanterns stretching the whole distance across the lawn, in spite of the fact that Halloween has been over for a couple of weeks now.

"Look out for the pumpkins!" I holler, hustling to the rescue.

She trips anyway, picks herself and the turkey up, and keeps on coming as if nothing happened. I take the turkey from her, and she brushes off her pea green velvet jogging suit. "Mr. Coolidge does love those pumpkins," she says, smiling.

"That is true," Mr. Coolidge agrees. "We can leave our pumpkins in the capable care of our Pilgrims and Indians until we get back from Illinois."

"Back from Illinois?" Catman repeats.

"We're going to Nice? Crashing at Uncle Chester's pad?"

"We are indeed," Mr. Coolidge answers.

"I can dig it." Catman high-fives me.

I'm glad they're going to help out at the Rescue. "You'll be back in time for Thanksgiving though, right? Lizzy's already been working out the menu." I don't add that she's taken on a third babysitting job to fund Thanksgiving dinner for everybody. It will be the first time Catman's family and mine have gotten together for Thanksgiving.

Mrs. Coolidge turns to me and frowns. "Oh, dear. In all the hubbub, I forgot about our previous commitment. Oh my. We promised to give Bart's brother and his family as much help as we can with that barn. And I volunteered to cook their Thanksgiving meal. I don't mean to be unkind, but my sister-in-law has trouble heating frozen dinners in the microwave."

"You'll be gone on Thanksgiving Day?" I ask, hoping I'm getting it wrong.

"I told the girls at the beauty parlor we'd be gone all week. And Mr. Coolidge got Stanley to take over for him at the car lot. Dear, dear, dear, dear, dear . . . Do you think your family will mind so very much if we're not there for Thanksgiving? I hope I haven't hurt anyone's feelings."

A pang of disappointment shoots through me. You'd think I'd be used to disappointment by now, but this one still hurts. "Don't worry about it, Mrs. Coolidge. No big deal." I smile and try to sound like I mean it. "It's great that you can help out like that." I edge closer to Nickers and put my arm over her neck. She lifts her head, still munching the long grass that sticks out from her lips like green straws.

Mrs. Coolidge takes off her mittens, puts them on a young plastic Pilgrim girl, then wrings her hands. "Well, I do hope the new Mrs. Willis won't be terribly upset with us."

My dad and Madeline have been married for three years, but Mrs. Coolidge still calls Madeline the new Mrs. Willis. "She'll understand. So will Lizzy. Lizzy's the cook in our house."

"Well," Mr. Coolidge chimes in, "we felt it incumbent on ourselves at this time of year to offer assistance in the great task of rebuilding that shelter before winter sets in."

"You're absolutely right to go," I agree. And I do mean it. "Those horses need stalls before winter sets in. I wish *I* could do something to help."

"Right on!" Catman exclaims, those intense blue eyes of his locking on me. "Road trip for the whole Willis clan! Out of sight!"

I shake my head at him. "You, Catman Coolidge, are not the most practical person I know. There's no way my family could take off on a trip like that. Dad's lined up odd jobs with some of his old clients over the holidays. He's booked all week. Lizzy's doing extra baby-sitting duty. Besides, we could never afford a trip like that right now."

"Sa-a-ay! Speaking of trips," Mr. Coolidge begins, "why did the chicken cross the mean streets of Ohio?"

I laugh because sometimes it's easier to laugh in the middle of his jokes than it is after he's delivered the punch line.

Mr. Coolidge pats his toupee like he always does before the punch line. "So he could drive a Smart Bart's used car to Nice! Get it? *Nice*, Illinois? *Mean* streets?"

Mr. Coolidge is the proud owner of Smart Bart's, and most of his jokes are about his used-car business.

Mrs. Coolidge kisses her husband's forehead. "I am a lucky woman, Mr. Coolidge." She turns to me. "Winnie, did you get your college applications sent in?"

"Not yet," I answer. I don't look at Catman. He knows about my change in plans, but he still tells everybody that he and I are going to Ohio State. Apparently he hasn't even told his parents that I'll be taking classes at the local community college instead of going to OSU.

"Now don't fret, my love," Mr. Coolidge says. He takes off his Yosemite Sam necktie and wraps it around the Pilgrim father's neck. "No veterinary school would dare turn down Winnie the Horse Gentler."

Mrs. Coolidge laughs like she agrees that turning me down from vet school would be ridiculous. "Did Calvin tell you he got three acceptance letters last week?"

I frown at him, but he's playing with Churchill, his flat-faced, giant gray cat. "Catman never said a word, Mrs. Coolidge."

"Harvard pre-law, George Washington University pre-med, and UCLA psychology," Mr. Coolidge reports. "That's not counting that film school in New York City that heard about his cat documentary."

"Wow!" I shouldn't be surprised. Catman and his buddy M aced every college prep test they threw at us. M is going to Oxford in England. He graduated early and moved overseas already. "Catman, congratulations. You should have told me."

He shrugs. "Not my bag. Still heading to Ohio State with you and Hawk. I should finish up the cat-umentary by late July."

"Hawk would love that," I counter, "especially since I'm backing out on her." Hawk was my best girlfriend until she moved away. I've really missed her. It would have been great to be roommates at OSU.

"Backing out? What do you mean, Winnie?" Mrs. Coolidge asks.

"I'm going to Ashland Community College. Not OSU. Didn't Catman tell you?" I know he didn't. But it's time he faced it. I've had to.

Nobody says anything.

"Do they have a veterinarian program?" Mrs. Coolidge asks, looking puzzled.

"No. I'm going into business," I explain.

"Somebody in our house has to learn to balance a checkbook." I force a laugh. "I'll always have horses. I know that. It's just . . . well . . . going into business makes more sense right now. I can live at home and help out more."

Catman won't look at me. We've gone round and round about this, but it's settled. And I'm okay with it. Really.

"But haven't you always wanted to be a vet, dear?" Mrs. Coolidge presses.

I shrug. "Sometimes things don't work out like you want them to. That's all."

"Say," Mr. Coolidge begins. I think we might be in for another joke, but then he says, "If your whole family can't get away to Nice, why don't *you* come with us, Winnie?"

"Far out!" Catman exclaims.

"You are the smartest man I know, Mr. Coolidge," his wife says.

For a second, I can see myself on a road trip with Catman. I'd get to meet everybody I've been e-mailing for so long. Then reality sets in again. And lately, reality equals money or the lack of it. I have zero money. I can't just go along without paying my part.

"Cool," Catman says, like I've agreed to go and it's all settled.

"Catman, I can't."

"Not dinero again," Catman says. "You're sweating no bread, true?"

I know he'll tell me that I don't need money. That he's got it covered. But I already owe him $43.10. I keep track.

Nickers stomps her hoof. Probably a fly.

"See?" I say, trying to make a joke of it. "Nickers doesn't want me to go. She put her foot down. My horse can't get along without me."

"Burg, Nelson, and Churchill have had to wing it without me most of this year, and they're cool to hang without *me* for a few more days, for a good cause," Catman counters.

"Not the same thing," I try.

"Because Nickers likes you more than Churchill and company like me?" Catman demands.

"No. I'm not saying that . . . not exactly."

He walks over and stares at me. "So, why can't you come with me? You know you want to." Catman knows me better than anybody else on earth.

"Catman Coolidge, you're the hardest person I know to say no to," I complain.

He cocks his head to the side, and his long blond ponytail slides over his shoulder. "Deep."

I elbow him in the chest, and he fake-falls backwards into the leaves and grass. The guy is twice as big as I am, but he acts like I hurt him. "Peace out, Willis," he begs. His big foot catches the back of my knee, and I tumble to the ground after him.

"You did that on purpose!" I grab a handful of fall leaves and throw them in his face.

Nickers doesn't like it. She tosses her head and whinnies at us.

"Children, children," Mrs. Coolidge scolds.

I lie on my back and stare at the blue sky. Wisps of white clouds float by. Geese honk overhead. Even if I did let them pay my way, I don't think Dad would go for it. He doesn't give much thought to money, but he refuses to owe anybody.

I gaze at Nickers, at her refined Arabian head, the perfect slope of her withers, her sleek white coat. She's so beautiful, inside and out. I wasn't kidding about not liking to be away from my horse.

Catman sits up. Leaves tumble off him. "Can't see leaving Nickers, can you?" he asks.

Sometimes I think Calvin "Catman" Coolidge reads my mind.

"So," he says, springing to his feet and sticking out his hand to give me a lift, "we won't."

"Why that's a wonderful idea, Calvin!" his mother exclaims.

"Indeed!" Mr. Coolidge agrees.

Note to self: No matter how much time I spend with the Coolidges, I'll never be able to read their minds.

"Who's going to tell me what I'm missing here?" I ask.

Before I know what hit me, Catman hoists me over his shoulder in a fireman's carry.

"Catman!"

He spins me around, then dumps me into a pile of leaves. "Nickers," he says, "is coming with us."

ELEVEN

FOR A MINUTE I'm totally psyched. A road trip with Catman and Nickers? A chance to meet Kat, Dakota, and Wes? And maybe I could help Hank with Cleopatra.

Then reality sets in. What about gas? Our horse trailer gets horrible mileage. To haul Nickers out to Illinois would cost more than I'd make in months shoveling manure at Spidells' Stable-Mart. And what about food on the way? And expenses once we got there? My food *and* Nickers's grain.

Life was so much easier when I was

younger, when I just believed things would work out in spite of reality, in spite of everything.

"Come on. Let's clue in your old man," Catman says.

"I haven't agreed to anything. I'm pretty sure Dad won't want me to go."

He totally ignores me and whistles for Nickers.

My horse stops grazing and stares at him. I think she's laughing. Then she goes back to munching grass.

"Nickers?" I call.

Nickers trots toward me, and I swing onto her back. "I wish I *could* go to Nice, but I can't. You have to see that, right?"

Catman steps onto the old stump we use as a mounting block and waits until Nickers and I sidle up to it. His steady grin is his way of saying he's not paying attention to me this time.

We ride in silence to my house, but it feels like we're arguing. Catman can say more without words than most people can say with words.

When we're halfway up the road to my house, Catman mutters something. I think he says, "Funky, man."

I follow where he's looking and see Dad

and Madeline struggling with a tall metal pole that fans out like an upside-down umbrella. Skinny ropes dangle from the top.

"New invention?" Catman whispers to me.

"Looks like it," I whisper back. "Hope this one sells better than the last one."

"The parent saddle? That one was far out, man."

"It was *too* far out. The licensing people told Dad that parents don't give their kids horsey rides anymore."

Madeline's last invention was a dining table that opened into a dishwasher so you wouldn't have to get up from the table to clear it. That's the one that just about broke us.

Dad calls when we ride up on the lawn. "What's the word from your cousin?"

"Still a bad scene, but it wasn't arson," Catman answers. To me, he whispers, "Are you cluing him in on the road trip, or am I?"

"Catman," I whisper, "I told you I can't–"

"Well," Madeline says, "I guess that's one good thing, knowing that nobody set the fire on purpose. I hope you'll tell the family we're praying for them."

"Catman!" Mason rushes to us as soon as

we're on the ground. Mason's my little brother. We got him when we got Madeline, which made it all worth the effort, if you ask me. He's small for his age. And he's sweet for his age because his mind doesn't always work the way most people's minds work.

"Be right back," I tell Mason. "I need to cool Nickers down. How was Buddy today?" Buddy is Mason's horse. We've had her for almost five years. She was born right here in our barn.

"I brushed her shiny," Mason says, grinning. He grabs Catman's hand and tugs him toward the house.

I say hey to Buddy, then brush Nickers and cool her down. All the while, I'm bracing myself for what I know Dad will say when Catman tells him about the trip. Dad will tell him I can't go. And I understand. Even if Dad turned out to be okay with Catman's family paying for everything, it would still mean I wouldn't be bringing home a paycheck from Spidells' Stable-Mart. I already told Dad I put in for extra hours over Thanksgiving break.

I turn Nickers out to pasture, and when

I come back to the yard, Catman, Dad, and Madeline are laughing so hard they can't speak. "What?" I ask.

"Deep, man," Catman says. "It's not an invention."

"It's a clothesline!" Madeline cries, pointing to the contraption they've been struggling with.

Then Dad's laughter stops cold. "On the other hand, what if we put small wheels right here and here?"

Madeline stops laughing too. "Like roller skate wheels?"

"Exactly! I think this could be the next umbrella bike . . . maybe an umbrella skateboard!" Dad tugs at the cords. "We could get movable parts there."

"With three-quarter-inch screws on the ends!" Madeline adds.

"I was thinking wires," Dad suggests.

"You and your wires," Madeline counters. "What if we . . . ?"

I pull Catman away from the invention scene and into the house.

Note to self: So much for the clothesline. Prepare for wearing wet clothes.

Mason shoves into the house ahead of us. "Lizzy!" he yells. "Catman's here!"

"Thanks a lot, Mason," I call after him. "Aren't you forgetting somebody?"

He turns and smiles. "And Nickers!" he shouts.

I tousle his soft blond hair. "Yeah, well, *Buddy* was happy to see me."

Lizzy comes out of the kitchen with a big smile, as always. My "little" sister is half a foot taller than I am, twice as pretty, and three times as nice. If she were a horse, she'd be a noble and dependable Trakehner.

"Hey, you guys!" Lizzy presses a button, and a floor mat unrolls at Catman's feet. "Mind taking your shoes off, please?"

We kick off our shoes onto the mat. The roll-away welcome mat made us good money a couple of years ago, but imitations sprang up fast.

"How's Hank, Catman?" Lizzy asks. "I feel so bad for that family. Do they like caramel and candy canes? I'm experimenting with a new cookie recipe. Maybe I'll send them a care package."

We follow Lizzy to the kitchen. Our

kitchen looks like a cross between a sci-fi movie and a science lab. The fridge is really a counter with drawers. The cupboard looks like a fridge and turns like a lazy Susan. I don't know what half the dials and buttons do in this room.

Lizzy checks one of the ovens in her three-story oven. "Do you think your Illinois relatives would ever come here for Thanksgiving? I would love to cook for everybody! I've invented the coolest pumpkin dessert." She shuts that oven and opens the door to the oven above it. Something smells great in there. "Your uncle and everybody probably couldn't make it even if they wanted to, right? They'll have to rebuild the barn before winter, won't they?"

Catman raises his eyebrows, which means, "Yes."

"Thought so. Barker can't come either. They're having relatives in from all over. At least you'll be here." Lizzy taps lizard food into her dry lizard aquarium.

When Catman doesn't say anything, Lizzy spins around. "Catman?"

He twists his lips, which means, "Sorry."

"Why not?" she demands.

So we tell her. She nods and approves, but

I can tell she's disappointed. "Winnie's coming with us," Catman concludes.

"Catman!" I turn to Lizzy, whose green eyes are wide with surprise. "I'm not *really* going. I mean, I'd love to go and help with the horses and the barn and everything. But I know you guys need me to be here. And I'm working extra at the stable."

"Nickers is coming too," Catman continues, like I haven't just said I'm not going. "You should come, Lizzy."

"I'd love to." She's talking over my head to Catman, ignoring me like he is. "But I can't. I'll hold down the fort here, though. Barker and Pat can help me with the Pet Helpline." Lizzy sighs, then stands up from the table. "Time to talk to Dad."

"Wait a minute. I don't know if–," I begin. But nobody's listening to me. They're already out of the kitchen.

Lizzy leads the way to the clothesline, and Catman gets right down to it. "Need to rap with you cats," he announces. "The Nice Coolidges are totally bummed. So our Ohio crew plans to groove over there to make nice and do our thing. Can you dig it?"

Madeline and Dad look from Catman to each other. "What did he say?" Madeline asks.

Lizzy nods for me to interpret, but I shake my head. I've already given up on this trip to Nice. I should work at the stable. I don't want to ask for anything. Sometimes it's easier just to give it up. Life hurts less that way.

Lizzy takes over. "Winnie wants to go to Nice with Catman and his parents."

"And Nickers," Catman adds.

Dad scratches his head. "In our horse trailer?"

Lizzy nods.

Now Madeline scratches her head. She and Dad become more alike every day. Neither of them can sit still, and they'd both forget meals and bills if it weren't for Lizzy. "That trailer takes a lot of gas, doesn't it?" Madeline asks. "Isn't gasoline expensive these days?"

"It's a crazy idea," I say quickly. I wish Lizzy and Catman had kept their big mouths shut. "We shouldn't have asked."

I shouldn't have wanted it.

"Bread's no sweat," Catman says. "My folks won more gas coupons than we'd need to fly to the moon. Dad's grooving with jingles this year."

I know Catman's not making this up. His parents enter hundreds of contests and win plenty of them. One year they won a vacation to Bethlehem, Calcutta, Moscow, Paris, and a dozen other cities.

Turned out the cities were all in Ohio, but they had a great time.

"Tell them congratulations on winning another contest. That's simply wonderful!" Madeline exclaims. Her bright red hair is caught up in a clip that can't control it. She used to be as tall and skinny as my dad. She's still as tall, but Lizzy's cooking has turned her "pleasingly plump," as Lizzy puts it.

"We've got 83 boxes of granola for the trip," Catman continues. "Contests entries were on the backs. So no bread required for road chow."

Hope is trying to bubble up inside of me, but I squish it back down where it belongs. There's no way I could pull off this trip. What about the lost income from Spidells' Stable-Mart if I'm not here to muck stalls?

Dad turns to me. "Winnie, what do *you*

think? It seems to be up to you." This is the exact same thing he said when we found out how much it would cost for me to be a veterinarian. He didn't want to say no. He never wants to say no. But neither of us could see it happening.

Before I can answer, a car comes barreling up the drive, spraying gravel and squealing brakes. Mason runs to the barn. He hates loud noises.

Even before the dust settles and I see the gold convertible, I know it's Summer Spidell. Her dad owns the stable where I've worked off and on since we moved to Ohio. Summer used to ride, but she gave up horses the day her dad bought her a car.

Summer stops close to us and keeps the motor running. "Good. I caught you. You simply have to get a cell, Winnie. Daddy wants you. My brother's in town for the holidays, and they need you at the stable for who knows what. Daddy said to tell you that your extra hours start right now."

"Richard's back in town?" Ever since we've lived in Ashland, Summer and her brother have done everything they could to make my life miserable. With Richard off to college in California, at least I've had only Summer to deal with lately.

"Seriously," she whines, "you have to come. Daddy's threatening to make *me* clean stalls. Can you imagine? So, you *have* to get over there right this minute. If you don't and somebody actually saw me shoveling manure, I'd never be able to show my face again."

Summer Spidell, never show her face again? Some offers are too good to pass up.

I grin at Lizzy and Catman, then walk to the convertible and lean in until I'm face-to-face with Summer.

She backs away. "What are you doing?"

"Getting one last look at your face, Summer. 'Cause you're about to shovel manure for the entire Thanksgiving break. So I guess you won't be showing your face again."

"Right on!" Catman shouts.

"W-wait! Winnie!" Summer whines. "You *have* to do this. You don't understand. Maybe you can't muck stalls now. But surely over the break you can–!"

"No can do. I won't be here."

I'm not sure I've ever seen her this

desperate. "Why? Where are you going?" she demands.

"To a place I think it's safe to say you've never been. A place called Nice."

Hank Coolidge
Nice, Illinois

I TREAD SOFTLY OVER the wet leaves of the McCray pasture, inching toward Cleopatra as if she's surrounded by land mines. Yesterday Cleo bolted when I stepped on a twig. It's been over a week since the fire, and I still haven't gotten close enough to her to treat the burn on her rump. I know the vet took care of it when she sedated Cleo the night of the fire, but I'd like to see for myself how it's healing.

"Easy, Cleo," I murmur, inching through the tall weeds and over a fallen branch. It rained hard last night. I couldn't sleep, worrying about my horses having no good place to go for shelter. We put up a lean-to in the south pasture, but Cleo's got nothing here on the old McCray farm. She does have the basics—good water from the pond, enough grass among the weeds, a salt block I dropped off. She eats the oats I bring every day, but she waits until I'm gone to do it.

"I don't even want to catch you, Cleo," I mutter.

I learned from Winnie, my cousin Catman's friend, that the best way to catch a horse is to try *not* to catch her. "Horses don't like to be trapped or caught," she informed me the only time I met her, about three years ago when I went to Ashland with Gram. We spent a couple of days at Catman's. Winnie was pretty busy gentling a two-year-old Hanoverian for somebody, so we didn't spend much time with her. I did get to watch her in action one afternoon though. It was amazing. I learned a lot in those few hours. She's taught me even more through the Pet Helpline.

Only this time, this "pet" may be beyond help.

I close the distance between the mare and

me by walking diagonally and pretending that I'm heading for an invisible horse somewhere beyond Cleo. Horses have a fight-or-flight nature, and I've seen both with this sorrel.

My mind has replayed the fire a million times, especially the way I handled, or mishandled, Cleo. When I close my eyes, I still see Cleo cowered in the corner of her smoke-filled stall.

And I see the barn in flames. I don't think I'll ever get rid of that image.

I've also replayed everything I did in the days leading up to the fire. I've tried to pinpoint the last time I was in the loft. The last time I was on the roof. The last time I did a general check of the whole barn.

Since the fire inspector wrapped up his investigation, I've had time to do my own investigation of what used to be our barn. There are a lot of things I could have done better in the upkeep of that barn. I didn't go in the loft very often, not with the grass so good this year. If I'd checked our loft every day, maybe I would have seen a pinhole of light coming in from the roof. I might have seen water dripping in on the hay. Maybe I would have smelled mold and known the hay was turning combustible.

Now that everybody's so sure the fire wasn't some arsonist's fault, I want to know whose fault it was. I want to know if it was *my* fault.

When I'm about 15 yards from Cleopatra, her head springs up. Her ears flatten back, and her nostrils widen with fear. She snorts. I see her skin twitch, her muscles coil. She's ready to bolt if I take another step.

I don't.

I don't want to make this horse's life any worse than it already is.

I cross back the way I came, through the muddy pasture, down the ditch, and out to the road.

Dakota's waiting for me. She's got Blackfire saddled up western, which means she's going on a serious ride. "How's Cleopatra?" she asks.

"Don't ask me. I couldn't get close enough to her to tell. I think the burn's healing okay. Hard to say from here, though."

Blackfire dances in place, eager to get going.

"Well, Blackfire and I are celebrating the

start of fall break. Want to tag along for the ride? I think we'll go over by the quarry and look for Kitten again. Remember? That's where I found her the last time she disappeared."

"The barn wasn't on fire the last time she disappeared." There's no way that cat survived the fire. If I had any guts, I'd tell Kat what I think really happened instead of letting her go on hoping Kitten will magically turn up.

"Come on, Hank," Dakota pleads.

I shake my head. "Too much to do. Dad and I are starting work on the frame for the new barn this afternoon. He's got trucks coming out tomorrow to clear rubble."

"Sounds like you could use a break then," Dakota says. "I'm sure Starlight could. She misses you. She tried to follow Blackfire and me out of the pasture."

"Yeah, well, tell her I'm rebuilding the barn for her. She needs that more than she needs me. Starlight shouldn't have to stand outside in the rain. And I'm sure not going to make her stand out there in the snow. So I've got work to do."

"I don't think Starlight gets all that," Dakota says. "She just wants you to ride her."

"Look, Dakota. There's no time for Starlight."

"'No time for Starlight.' Sounds like the title of a cool book, but a sad state of affairs if you're a horse by the name of Starlight."

"Must be nice not to have to worry about all the work that needs to be done around here," I snap.

Dakota grins. "It's lovely." She and Blackfire trot down the lane.

I cut across two pastures on the way home and wish I'd stuck to the road. My jeans are soaking wet from the tall grass, and stickers cover me from the knees down. I slip crossing a ditch and end up mud-covered on my whole left side. Now I'll have to change clothes before I can get back to working on the barn.

I'm halfway up the drive when I see a blue Nissan next to the rubble. Someone's standing in the burned-down barn. I think she's taking pictures, maybe even shooting video.

"Hank!" Kat runs out of the house toward me.

"Not now, Kat." I walk faster toward the barn.

"I just need to ask you something!" Kat yells after me.

I wave her off. "Later. Somebody's out there."

I don't slow down until I reach the woman. I was right about the camera. She's holding one, and a second camera sits on a tripod a few feet behind her. "Hey! What are you doing out here?"

She looks up from her camera like *I'm* the intruder. "Excuse me?"

"Look." I take a deep breath and try to calm down. I thought we were done with the reporters crawling all over the place. "There's nothing left to report, okay? You need to go."

Frowning, the woman looks a lot older than I thought she was, more like Gram's age than Mom's. "And who exactly are you?" she asks.

"Who am *I*? I'm the one whose burned barn you're standing in. Who are *you*?"

"Ah," she says, dipping her head a little. "Sandra Leedy." She starts to stick out her hand but lets it drop to her side. "Didn't your father tell you I'd be finishing up today?"

"What?" The only thing I can think of

that might need finishing up is the fire investigation. "Are you with the fire investigation unit? Have they changed their minds about it not being arson?"

She takes a picture of a pile of ash where our round pen used to be. "No, no. I have a copy of the final report. They've ruled out arson. And I'm not with the county's fire unit."

"Then what are you—?"

"I'm sorry," she says, smiling. "Let's start over. Sandra Leedy with Farm Federal Insurance. I'm a claims investigator. You must be Mr. Coolidge's son." She sticks out her hand.

"Hank." I shake her hand. Her fingers are stiff and cold.

"Well, Hank, I should be out of your hair pretty soon. I think I've got all I need. I took most of the pictures yesterday and got my samples the day before. I'll be done today."

I can't believe Dad didn't even mention this to me. But I think I know why. "Insurance investigation. That means you're trying to find out if the fire's our fault, right? You want to prove it was our fault."

"Well, we wouldn't exactly put it that way in our brochure." She half laughs at her joke. "Insurance companies like to do their own follow-up investigations in cases like this before they pay out large sums of money for a claim."

"How long does that take?"

"Like I say, I'll finish up today. But it might be a couple of months before the evidence gets processed and returned from the lab."

"A couple of months?" I shout. "We need a barn now! Our horses can't wait on your investigation."

"I don't mean to say you can't do what you need to do until we're finished," she explains. "I probably shouldn't even be talking to you. Your father can fill you in." She stands there like she's waiting for me to leave so she can go back to doing whatever she was doing.

But I can't leave. I have to know if this fire was our fault, *my* fault. I need to know. I clear my throat and realize it's still sore, still burned.

Finally she says, "Look, I can tell you this much. If you're worried that I'll be citing negligence in my report, don't be."

"You mean it wasn't negligence? You don't think it was our fault?"

She looks at her notebook. "The lab results aren't back. But there's no sign of careless smoking or poor wiring, no flammables out in the open. You've passed every fire and safety inspection, and fire codes were up to par and then some." She smiles at me. "So you can stop worrying about that one. This fire wasn't your fault."

Not my fault. The fire was not my fault.

I know this should make me feel better. But it doesn't.

"I don't understand," I tell her. "If it's not arson and it's not our fault, then whose fault is it?"

She's already bending over the tripod to fold it up. "Hmm? Fault? Don't worry about that. This fire's a no-fault. We'll be writing it off as an act of God."

The words, pointed and jagged-edged, sink into me. *An act of God?*

What am I supposed to do with that?

THIRTEEN

Winnie Willis
Nice, Illinois

"WINNIE, WE'VE LANDED."

I hear the whisper in my dream. I feel someone's breath on my forehead, a hand smoothing my hair. Catman's hand, his breath. Only I don't know if I'm dreaming, or . . .

"Welcome to Nice," Catman says, louder this time.

I open my eyes, and I'm staring into Catman's piercing blue eyes. It takes me a few seconds to remember where I am—in the back-seat of the Coolidge-mobile. My head is on

Catman's shoulder. I must have been asleep for a while because it's dark out.

I sit up, suddenly embarrassed. "Sorry about that," I mutter.

"No sorrow here," Catman says. He leans up to the front seat. "That's the road, right there."

"Are you sure, Calvin?" his mother asks. "I can't tell in this dark." Mrs. Coolidge got her license only a couple of years ago. Since then, she gets behind the wheel whenever she can. I admit that I was a little nervous at first about Claire Coolidge hauling my horse and trailer behind the Coolidge-mobile, but she's actually done a great job. She takes the turn.

"Won't they be surprised!" Mr. Coolidge declares, straightening his tie.

"They will indeed," Mrs. Coolidge agrees.

"Wait." I'm really waking up now. "You mean you didn't tell them we were coming?"

"We did discuss Thanksgiving Day. Nothing else though." Catman's mother smiles into the rearview mirror. "Mr. Coolidge and I love surprises."

"But what if they've got other plans? What if they don't have room for *me*? Or for Nickers?" I've been nervous enough about spending the week with people I don't know. Put me with a dozen horses I've never seen before and I'm fine. But people? That's a totally different story. I've never been great around strangers, and it doesn't help to find out these people aren't even expecting us.

"Since early fall my brother and nephew have been lobbying for us to leave the sanctity of our Ohio abode and make a pilgrimage to the foreign soils of Illinois to celebrate Thanksgiving," Catman's dad says.

"They weren't lobbying to get Nickers and me here," I whisper to Catman.

"Peace out," Catman whispers back. "It's cool."

I press my nose to the cool window and stare at the stars. The black sky is filled with pinpricks of light. The gravel road changes to dirt. I peer through the back window at the trailer. It's too dark to make out Nickers inside, though. I can't wait to get her out of there.

We turn up a long drive. Yellow light spills from several windows of a big farmhouse. Unlike the Ohio Coolidge home, this one looks like it's in great shape. No boarded-up windows, no patched-up roof. And so far, no sign of a single plastic lawn ornament. "You're sure this is the right place?" I ask.

"Right on," Catman answers.

"The yard certainly is plain and undecorated," Mrs. Coolidge observes.

"Mother used to say *I* got the creativity in the family," Mr. Coolidge confides.

Catman turns to gaze out his own window. "Oh, man," he mutters. "Like, total bummer."

I pop my seat belt and slide over to peer out his window so I can see what he sees. Where a barn must have stood only a week ago, there's nothing but a pile of charred rubble. The horses were lucky to have lived through the fire, but they'll probably never be the same.

"Look! They're all outside!" Mr. Coolidge shouts. "I'll bet it's a moon check."

Catman explains, "Gram Coolidge started it. Anyone, anytime, can call a moon check, and the whole family has to chill out under the stars."

Catman and I have sat for hours on his roof and watched the stars in Ohio. Sometimes his parents climb out the second-story window and join us. Maybe we were doing our own

Ohio version of a moon check without real-izing it.

"Yes! There's Mother!" Mr. Coolidge exclaims.

His wife glances out her window, then taps the brakes until we come to a stop.

Several of the people stretched out across the lawn sit up and look our way. Mr. Coolidge reaches over and honks the horn. Then he lunges to get out, but he's still trapped in his seat belt.

"Here you go, dear." His wife unbuckles him. "Now, go give your mother a kiss."

Catman and I climb out of the backseat. My stomach is knotting up the way it always does when I'm around new people. "Go on ahead," I tell him. "I need to get Nickers unloaded. I haven't stretched her since Indiana."

"I'll help," he volunteers.

"No thanks. I got it. Go say hi to your cousins and grandmother and everybody." I give him a nudge.

He grabs my hand, squeezes it, then takes off running, racing past his parents to the Coolidge crowd. Catman knows me well enough to understand that I need to be with

Nickers before I face the masses. I watch him run straight to an older woman, wrap his arms around her, and spin her around. I'm guessing it's his grandmother. I met her a few years ago when she came to Ashland to visit. What I remember most is her palomino hair. That, and the fact that she scared me a little until I realized she was extremely nice but extremely bossy. She struck me as a cross between a classy thoroughbred and a tough-skinned barb.

My eyes adjust to the semidarkness as I move to the back of the trailer. "Easy, Nickers," I say, working the trailer latch. "I'll get you out of there in no time." She shuffles her hooves when I swing the doors open.

It's a two-horse trailer, and my plan is to climb the ramp, walk through the empty half, and get my horse. I tug on the tailgate ramp, but the thing won't budge. I pull at it again. It's been stuck before, but it just can't be stuck now. I want my horse.

"Need some help?"

I turn to see a dark-haired girl who's almost as beautiful as Lizzy. Her hair is wild and curly. She's slim and a couple of inches taller than I am. If she were a horse, she might be an Andalusian, an elegant Spanish horse with big eyes and inner strength. I recognize her from the news clip. "Dakota?"

"That's me."

I don't know if I should hug her or shake her hand or what. We've been friends in cyber-space, exchanging dozens of e-mails, spending time on the Pet Helpline. But this is different. "I'm Winnie," I announce stupidly.

"You're kidding," she says.

"No, I'm–" I stop, finally getting the sar-casm. She had it in cyberspace too.

"You look pretty much like your e-mails," Dakota says, grinning. "Maybe a little shorter."

I laugh. I like her already.

"So, need any help?" Dakota asks.

"I could use some help," I admit, grateful to have something to do besides try to talk. "I can't get the ramp to come down." I step aside and let Dakota try. Then we both pull, and it moves a little on one side, but it still won't come down.

Dakota shouts toward the house, "Wes! Come here!"

Wes appears so fast that I think he must

have been watching us from behind the tree. With him comes a big dog who looks friendly enough. But Nickers isn't used to dogs, and she's never been that crazy about them. I think she'll be okay as long as the dog doesn't start barking.

"What's up?" Wes nods a greeting at me, then walks up to the stuck ramp.

"Thanks." I feel like I should say something else to him, but I have no idea what. I wish Lizzy were here.

The three of us tug at the same time, and the ramp pulls free, making us stumble backwards.

"Thanks," I tell them. There's an awkward silence, and again I know I should say more, but I don't know what to say. Where's my sister when I really need her? Lizzy can talk the spots off a Pinto.

Loud voices are coming from the Coolidge gathering a few yards off. I can't tell if they're happy or angry. I start up the trailer ramp, then turn back to Wes and Dakota. "Um . . . you guys didn't know we were coming, right? You think it's okay we're here?"

"Okay by me," Dakota says.

"Me too," Wes agrees. He does some kind of finger motion, and his dog runs to him and sits at his feet.

Dakota smiles. "You should have seen Kat's face when Catman ran up."

"He was looking forward to meeting Kat too," I tell them. "And her cats. And you guys. And seeing Hank. I guess they haven't been together for a couple of years. What did Hank say?"

I catch the look exchanged between Wes and Dakota. Then she shrugs. "I don't know. Hank didn't come out for the moon check."

Nickers paws the floor, shaking the whole trailer. She whinnies. Somewhere in the distance, a horse answers her.

"I better get her out." I make my way to my horse. "Easy, girl. I'm right here." I snap on the lead rope and back her down the ramp with no problem.

Now that she's out, with solid ground under her hooves, she can't stand still. I feel the tension coursing through her like electricity as she picks up strange scents, sights, and sounds.

"She's gorgeous," Dakota says. "Arabian, right? Is she high-strung?"

"No," I snap. I don't mean to be so defensive, but too many people have misjudged my horse. Lizzy says I'm way too sensitive when it comes to Nickers. "Nickers is high-spirited," I explain, "but I couldn't ask for a better horse." She's sidestepping now, and her nostrils are big as she takes in the new smells. "She's kind of wound up from the journey, I guess."

"I think Blackfire has some Arabian in him," Dakota says. "You'll have to see him tomorrow. He's out in the south pasture with a couple of the rescues."

I want her to tell me where I can put Nickers. If I could lead Nickers around the grounds, she'd calm down. But I don't know the lay of the land here, and it's too dark to explore. Nickers eyes Wes's dog. My horse's ears flatten back. I turn her in a circle to try to get her mind off the dog.

"Come over and meet everybody!" Catman's mother yells.

"Weird seeing more Coolidges," Wes says. "Popeye and his brother sure do look alike."

"Couldn't be because they're twins, could it?" Dakota says.

"I know that," Wes fires back.

"Dakota! Wes? Winnie?" somebody shouts in a high-pitched voice.

"That's Gram Coolidge," Dakota explains. "We better get over there." She and Wes walk toward the Coolidge crowd that's gathered on the other side of the house, closer to the burned-out barn.

I follow as far as the edge of the house, but Nickers doesn't want to get any nearer to that barn. She snorts and prances. She's being a real handful.

Note to self: Why did I bring Nickers here? Why did Catman bring me here? What on earth were we thinking?

I circle Nickers to calm her down, but she's still tense.

Catman trots over to us. "Far out, huh? Wait till you meet little Kat. She's grooving to meet you."

"Nickers is pretty wound, Catman."

He reaches to scratch Nickers's neck, but she sidesteps.

"Greetings!" hollers a man who looks exactly like Catman's dad, minus the toupee and tie.

"Winnie," Catman says, "this is my uncle Chester."

"You were right, Catman. That's the finest horse I've ever seen, and that's the prettiest Ohioan I've ever seen." He grins at me.

"Right on," Catman agrees.

I elbow Catman. "Thanks for having us. I hope we won't be too much trouble."

"Nonsense!" he protests. "We'll put you to work. The way Catman talks, there's nothing you can't do."

I don't know what to say, which is nothing new for me.

"Popeye!" Wes hollers.

"That's me," Catman's uncle says. "Guess I'm wanted." He walks off.

I watch him go, and already I feel better. I'm not sure if it's because Catman's uncle is so nice or because Catman said Nickers and I were pretty.

A door slams, and a tall figure storms out of the house. Behind him is a shaggy, limping dog. "What's going on out here?" he shouts.

He's too loud. Nickers picks up on the energy and dances in place again.

"Hank! Hey, man!" Catman runs up to his

cousin and hugs him, somehow managing to lift him off the ground. The little dog yaps at Catman's heels.

Nickers is getting more antsy by the minute. I circle her and move closer to the house so I can hear what Catman and Hank are saying.

"No, it's great to see you, too, Catman," Hank says, not sounding convincing.

I'm not sure I would have recognized Hank Coolidge. He's a lot taller than the last time I saw him. I remember having the overall impression of Hank as an easygoing cowboy, but he doesn't fit that description at all now.

"Been too long, man!" Catman play-punches Hank's arm.

"I know," Hank says. "It's just . . . I wish you'd picked a better time to visit. We've got a lot of work to do on the barn and—"

Nickers paws the ground.

Hank wheels on Nickers and me. "What's that?"

"Winnie and her horse," Catman answers.

"You've got to be kidding!" He runs his fingers through his hair. "Where are we supposed to put another horse? We don't have places for the horses we've got. I've got three horses crowded into one pasture already. We don't have a barn, in case you haven't noticed."

I feel awful. This is exactly what I was afraid of. "Nickers is fine without a barn," I tell him.

Hank says something, but I can't hear him because the limping dog starts yapping again. Wes's big dog trots up to Hank and barks.

Nickers is startled. She jerks back. I'm not ready for it. The rope slips through my fingers. She rears.

"Easy, Nickers," I say. "Stand down."

She does. She stops rearing, but her whole body is quivering.

Hank charges toward us, bringing the barking dogs with him.

Nickers bolts, but I grab the rope in time. She rears again.

"Stay back, will you?" I yell at Hank. My heart is pounding. I can feel Nickers's fear. I hate seeing my horse like this. She rode all the way here, and now this?

"Down, Nickers," I urge.

She comes down from her rear. The rope slacks. She touches ground, then lunges back. I can't hold on to the rope. Nickers pivots, then gallops off, disappearing into the darkness.

"Great." Hank spits out the word. "That's all we need around here. Another wild horse." He turns his back to me and says to Catman, "I can't believe you'd bring that wild thing with you."

Wild Thing? That's what people used to call my horse before she and I became best friends. It's what Summer Spidell still calls her.

And I will not stand for it. I grab Hank's arm and spin him around. He's so tall I have to crane my neck to look at him. "My horse is not a 'wild thing.' Her name is Nickers."

Then I push past him and run as fast as I can after my horse.

Note to self: Next time, stay home and shovel manure.

FOURTEEN

I SLEEP IN LATE THE NEXT MORNING. It didn't take me long to catch up with Nickers last night. Dakota helped. We brought her back close to the house and settled her in the paddock. Dakota waited with me until I was sure Nickers would be okay on her own there.

After that, Dakota, Kat, and I stayed up talking most of the night in Kat's room. It was pretty cool. I've never done that with anybody except Lizzy and Hawk. I slept in Kat's spare bed, and Dakota camped out in a sleeping bag on Kat's floor. When I woke up, I had a three-legged dog on my pillow. Kat had four cats on her bed. And Dakota was gone.

Catman is standing over the stove when I come downstairs. His dad and uncle are sitting across from each other at the dining room table. They're holding their newspapers in the exact same way, folded over three times. It freaks me out a little to see two Mr. Coolidges.

"Morning, everybody," I call, joining Catman in the kitchen.

"Good morning to you, Winnie!" Mr. Chester Coolidge and Mr. Bart Coolidge declare in unison, as if they've rehearsed it.

"Toasted peanut butter and cheese sandwich?" Catman offers. "With fresh tomatoes?"

I'm used to his weird food creations. "No thanks." I watch him flip the sandwiches like they're pancakes. "Where is everybody?"

"Dakota said to tell you she's in the south pasture," Catman says. "Everybody else split before I got down here."

"My Annie is at the hospital saving lives," Catman's uncle reports.

For a second I think he says *Miami*. Then I realize he's talking about his wife.

"Wes is at Nice Manor, the assisted-living

home," he continues. "He's planning some kind of dog show or dog training event with them to raise money for the barn. Awfully proud of that young man."

"Kat was telling me about the fund-raising plans last night," I say. "Her Fur Ball sounds great too. Sorry we're going to miss that one."

That accounts for everybody with the exception of Hank. I'm not looking forward to my next encounter with him. He's so different than he sounded in his e-mails. And he's changed a lot since he was in Ashland. Or maybe I never really got to know him. "So, where's Hank, Mr. Coolidge?" I ask, trying to sound casual.

"Better call me Popeye," he answers, "to avoid confusing me with my little brother."

"A matter of minutes," his twin protests.

"Wes dubbed me Popeye, and it's stuck."

"Popeye it is, then," I agree.

"Let's see. . . . I believe Hank's gone into town to get a few supplies and to pick up more lumber. I don't expect him back for quite a while."

"Good," I mutter.

"What was that, Winnie?" Popeye asks.

Catman jumps to the rescue. "She said, 'Good.' Like, it's groovy to see the barn getting rebuilt."

"Did Hank tell you the guys at the station house are all coming to help us raise the barn?" Popeye asks.

"Far out!" Catman says. "A real barn raising?"

Popeye pours himself and his brother another cup of coffee, then sits down again. "I am blessed with some great buddies in the department."

"My brother always did have a grand array of friends," Catman's dad observes.

"Morning." Kat breezes in so silently she could be a ghost. Or an angel. Her bright red wig doesn't quite fit the angel image, but the rest of her does. She's thin and graceful, almost breakable, with a kind of see-through skin that shows her veins. Her eyes are soft, like they've seen things the rest of us haven't. Last night she took off her wig to go to bed, and she talked so openly about her cancer that she put me at ease.

"Morning, Kat!" the Coolidge twins call in unison.

Kat walks to the porch and lets her cats outside, then joins Catman and me in the kitchen. She wrinkles up her nose when she gets close. "Something smells funny." When she sees the peanut butter, tomato, and cheese sandwich, her face goes even whiter. She swallows hard. "Catman?"

"Yes I am." Catman slides two sandwiches on small plates and delivers them to the Coolidge twins.

"When can we start looking for Kitten?" Kat asks, as Catman flips a final sandwich onto his own plate.

I catch a troubled look pass between the Coolidge twins. I have a feeling they both believe that cat's gone for good, burned up in the fire.

"Honey," Kat's dad begins, "Catman might not have time to—"

"Solid," Catman says. "I'm here for a cat hunt, as promised. But first I need to ask you some questions, Kat." He moves to the dining table and plops down next to his uncle. He waits until Kat and I take seats across from him. Then he asks Kat, "Have you looked for Kitten in the usual digs? Checked her secret pads?"

Kat nods. "I keep checking her favorite spots over and over. I climbed the oak tree out front. She loves that tree. I've checked the basement, my closet, the old shed where Dad parks the mower. We drove to the quarry because that's where Dakota found her when she ran away last summer. I've looked everywhere. Everyplace except the barn."

We're all quiet. I don't know about the others, but I'm imagining Kat discovering her burned-up cat in the burned-out barn. I shake my head to get rid of the image.

Catman swallows his last bite of sandwich and stares at Kat. "Okay then."

"Okay then?" Kat stares back at Catman.

"We'll have to find your cat from the inside out, not the outside in." He pops up from the table and puts his empty plate into the sink.

Kat follows him. "Inside out?"

He turns the full power of those intense blue eyes on Kat. "I'll need you to tell me everything about your cat. Can you do that?"

"Yes!" Kat's eyes are as big as Catman's and filled with admiration.

I get up from the table. "Sounds to me like you're in good hands, Kat. I think I'll go find Dakota and see how Nickers is getting along."

"Wait!" Popeye cries. "What's the hardest part about learning to ride a horse?"

"Learning to ride a horse?" I repeat, wondering if he's hinting that he'd like to learn to ride.

"What's the hardest part about learning to ride a horse? The ground!" he cries, answering his own riddle. "Get it?"

I laugh. I should have known. Bad jokes must run in the family.

"'The horse hooves pound. I hit the ground. We pass a hound who barks a sound.' That's from a little children's book I'm working on." Popeye's face turns pink. I think he's blushing.

"Sounds good," I tell him.

"What's the best story to tell a runaway horse?" he asks quickly, before I can reach the door.

I shake my head. "I give, Popeye."

"What's the best story to tell a runaway horse? A tale of *whoa*!" The answer comes in stereo—from Popeye and from his brother.

"Still telling those same old jokes, I see," Bart Coolidge accuses.

Popeye smiles at me. "This man, as you must know by now, is king of the bad joke."

"Sa-a-ay," Bart begins, "why did the Ferris wheel cross the road?"

I think Popeye is about to answer when Bart beats him to it. "Because it heard that Smart Bart's Used Cars is *wheel* friendly!" He cracks up, laughing so hard he ends in a coughing fit.

Kat laughs until there are tears in her eyes. Then she stops and runs to the window. She pulls back the cat curtain. "Hank's coming up the drive."

That's my cue. I slip on my jacket and sneak out while I can.

FIFTEEN

BEFORE HANK SHUTS OFF the truck's engine, I'm in the paddock with Nickers. Hank doesn't see me, or maybe he pretends not to. Fine with me.

"Hey, Nickers," I call. Her head springs up, and she's at attention—neck arched, ears pricked forward. I never get tired of looking at my horse. Watching her stirs something inside of me.

Nickers prances over, and I wrap my arms around her neck and press my cheek to her soft fur. She nickers without sound, letting me feel the gentle vibration of it in her throat. "I missed you too," I tell her.

Around us the farm has taken on a whole different look in the morning light. A few trees still reflect every color of orange, red, yellow, and brown. There's a musky smell from the damp, fallen leaves in the pasture, but I can smell smoke, too. A breeze blows in chilly air, but it's still warmer than Ohio.

I scratch Nickers's jowl right where she likes it. Her eyelids droop to half-mast with pleasure.

At the far end of the paddock, on the other side of the fence, Dakota appears, leading a black horse. She walks along the fence until she's opposite Nickers and me. "Morning," she calls. She's wearing jeans and a jean jacket, and I never would have guessed she grew up in Chicago if she hadn't told me so.

"Is this Blackfire?" I ask her. The gelding is black as night, without a single white marking. "He's amazing. Everything you said he was and more."

She nods, playing it cool, but her dimples give away how proud she is of that horse. "Blackfire and I finished our ride, but we could go again if you want to ride Nickers."

I do. There's nothing I want more than

to take off on Nickers. But I know that's not why I'm here. "Maybe later," I finally answer. "I feel like I should take a look at Cleopatra first. Where is she, anyway?"

"About a mile from here. If you can wait for me to brush Blackfire and take him back to his pasture, I'll show you where we've got Cleo."

I get Nickers's brushes from the trailer, and we groom Blackfire and Nickers right where they are, on opposite sides of the paddock fence.

"Thanks," Dakota says, handing back the brushes. "All our brushes burned in the fire. Hank replaced a couple, but I liked the old ones better."

"I'm really sorry, Dakota."

"Not your fault. Let's go see Cleo."

We tromp through high grass and across ditches and pastures. We're pretty quiet as we walk along together. Again, I wish Lizzy were here. She'd have Dakota talking a blue streak in no time.

"So," Dakota tries, "it must be great to be a senior."

"It's okay," I answer.

"Yeah," she presses. "At least it has to be

cool knowing you're headed for Ohio State next year. Not that I'm crazy about school or anything, even a party school. I'm just saying it would be sweet knowing all the studying was going for a good cause—to learn more about horses and how to help them. You probably have to take a bunch of regular classes first though, right? Before you get to the real veterinarian classes? That would stink. But it would be worth it to end up a vet."

"I'm not," I tell her.

"Not what?"

"Not everything. I'm not going to OSU. I'm not going into a pre-vet program. And I'm not going to be a vet."

"But that's what Kat said. Catman told her you were—"

"Catman was wrong."

Dakota frowns at me. "I don't get it. I thought you've always wanted to be a vet."

"I did. But it costs a lot of money to become a vet. My family doesn't have money."

"But if God wants you to be a vet, won't the money come from somewhere?" Dakota asks this so sincerely that I'm not sure how to answer her. I know that when she came to

Starlight, she didn't believe in God or anything else. So she hasn't had her faith very long. "It's not that easy, Dakota."

"But why not? God's in charge, right? Kat showed me a verse that says nothing's impossible with God. Something like that. And there's that one about God giving us the desires of our hearts. I love that verse. Being a vet is still the desire of your heart, right?"

"Yeah," I admit. "I guess. I mean, I've always wanted to be a vet. But the older you get, the more you start seeing that things are complicated. My family couldn't even pay the electric bill last week. How can I squeeze out money to go to OSU and then vet school? It's just not going to happen."

"But if you pray and believe, it could, right?" Dakota asks. "Because God loves you and wants the best for you and everything? Isn't that how it works?"

I don't know how to explain it to her. She's so new. Everything about her faith is still simple and straightforward. I remember feeling like that, like all I had to do was believe, and God would take care of the rest. It would be great to feel like that again. I still love God and everything. And I know He loves me. It's just different now.

"There's Cleo," Dakota says.

I'm grateful to have the subject changed.

At the far end of an overgrown pasture stands a lanky sorrel whose beauty can't be hidden by the burrs in her tail or the wild look in her eyes. She's not grazing. Her whole body says she's watching us, expecting the worst.

My heart aches for the damaged mare. "That poor horse."

"What are you going to do?" Dakota asks. "Hank hasn't been able to get anywhere near her since the fire. And he wasn't doing all that great before the fire."

"So the horse is as intelligent as she is beautiful," I mutter, the sting of him calling my horse Wild Thing still fresh in my mind.

"Hank's not usually like this," Dakota says.

"For your sake, I hope not." I climb the fence, and she climbs over after me.

"Hank feels responsible for rebuilding the barn before winter hits," Dakota explains. "He's a pretty intense guy, and he can't see how he's going to pull it all off, even with the whole fire department coming to help."

"You're right," I admit, feeling a little guilty for being so down on Hank. "I don't really know Hank. I met him one time. I shouldn't have said anything. Anyway, we've got more important things to work out."

We lean against the fence and watch Cleopatra. Her eyes are fixed on us.

"Look at those worry lines above her eyes," I observe. "Even her eyelids are wrinkled."

A twig snaps somewhere behind her, and the mare bolts sideways. Her nerves and muscles are on high alert.

"We'll need to make the pasture smaller." I'm pretty much thinking out loud. "It doesn't have to be round, but I need a safe area, like a round pen."

"We had one in the barn," Dakota says. "Maybe we could borrow some of the lumber Hank's got stacked up for the barn frame. We could block off the tip of this pasture pretty easily."

"Good. Remember how you played music to help calm Blackfire when you soaked his hoof to get rid of that abscess? I'd like Cleo to be treated to music when we're out here. She'll like the music, so that should take the edge off every time we show up. We'll be bringing her something she likes."

"Sweet. I'll take care of the music," Dakota promises.

"We need to be around this horse as much as possible from now on. You and I can take turns sitting out here and reading to her or singing or whatever it takes. But she needs to get the idea that not all humans are threatening."

"Hey, I'm up for it. Totally." She clears her throat. "Um . . . Hank could be a bit of a problem."

"Why? Because we want to help his horse?" My anger at Hank comes flooding back fast.

"Not that," Dakota says quickly. "It's just that I told him I'd help with the barn."

I turn to her. "Dakota, I'm going to shoot straight with you. From what I've seen of Cleopatra, she's as shell-shocked as any horse I've ever worked with. Maybe even Nickers."

"Nickers?" Dakota asks. "Was your horse really this far gone?"

I stare at Cleo while I explain what my horse was like when I first met her. "People called her Wild Thing, and back then, the name fit. The first time I saw that white Arabian, she galloped through a mist, leading a pack of horses behind her. Nobody could get near her. The biggest stable in Ashland, Spidells' Stable-Mart, picked her up at an auction, and they only made things worse." I turn to face Dakota. "It took me weeks and weeks to make friends with Nickers. And I've only got a few days with Cleo."

"I guess I didn't realize how bad off Cleo is," Dakota mutters, her voice breaking.

"Fire gives horses a kind of terror they don't get anywhere else," I explain. "And every day that horse is left on her own, she gets farther and farther away from human contact and deeper and deeper into herself. Pretty soon, nobody and nothing will be able to reach her. I need you here with me, Dakota."

"Then this is where I'll be," Dakota says. "Hank will have to understand."

Note to self: And if he doesn't, then it's just too bad for him.

Sixteen

Hank Coolidge
Nice, Illinois

"How's it going, Kat? Settling in okay, Catman?" I try to sound casual and friendly as I trudge by my sister and cousin for the 10th time on my way to the barn. Each time I pass the porch loaded down with two-by-fours or bags of cement, they're still lounging on the step in exactly the same spot.

Catman doesn't look away from Kat, but he raises one hand, fingers in a V, the universal sign for peace.

Like peace is an option with all this work to do? Not for me, it's not.

Since Catman and crew arrived three days ago, I've spent every minute of daylight working on the barn frame. Mom, Dad, Aunt Claire, and Uncle Bart have worked too. Even Wes pitched in before he took on more dogs for dog-sitting money. Dakota's helped a lot, but she spends most of her time with Winnie. And I don't even want to know what Winnie's doing. So I don't ask.

But Catman? He hasn't hammered a single nail since he's been here.

I stumble and drop the bag of cement I'm hauling to the barn. White powder puffs out and floats over me like ash. It's the last straw.

I stomp back to Catman. "You know, this barn isn't going to build itself."

Kat frowns at me. "I thought Dad's firemen buddies were coming to help with a big barn raising and everything."

I check my anger because this is Kat. "They're coming, all right." I turn to Catman and try not to clench my teeth. "But if we don't get the frame done first, there won't be anything for them to raise."

Catman shades his eyes when he squints at me. "Deep."

It takes everything in me not to go off on him. "Catman, in case you haven't noticed, we have a whole barn to rebuild!"

"Dude," Catman says calmly, "you've got more than a barn to rebuild."

I storm to the barn, hoisting the bag of cement onto my shoulder, before I say something I might regret. I've waited for years for Catman to come out and visit us, and now I can hardly wait until he leaves.

Dakota is still hammering on her part of the frame when I get back to the barn. She's been there for over an hour. She sits on her heels and points to a bag of nails next to her. "Are these the ones you wanted from the truck?"

They're not. "I needed the bigger ones, the spikes."

She hops up. "Aye, aye, captain. Be right back." She jogs toward the truck.

I take over her hammer and examine what she's done. The nails are straight and right on target.

"Here you go," she says, dropping a big bag of spikes. "So where's Popeye?"

I arrange the next section of two-by-fours on the ground. "Dad got called into the fire station before dawn. He woke up Uncle Bart and took him along for the ride. I wish they'd get back since nobody else is around to help." I hammer in the first spike. It feels good to slam it into the wood.

"Everybody's doing what they can," Dakota says.

"Right," I say with all the sarcasm I can muster. "Catman sits around all day talking cats to Kat. Winnie the Great Horse Gentler disappears all day to play with the horses."

"That's not fair, Hank."

"Really?" I bang in another spike in three swings. "So what exactly is the great horse whisperer doing this morning? Reading to Cleo? Singing to her?"

"Well," Dakota says, "whatever it is, it's working."

"Yeah? Doesn't seem like it's working to me. Let's see. . . . Has she brushed the horse yet? Treated that burn, maybe?"

"No," Dakota admits. "But Cleo's coming closer and closer to check things out. I don't think she's afraid of Winnie anymore. And we tried something new last night."

She waits for me to beg her for the newest

secret technique of Winnie the Horse Gentler. I hammer another spike. I get it in two swings this time.

"Laughter," Dakota says.

That stops me. I stare at Dakota. "Laughter?"

"I'm not kidding you. Winnie must have laughed for two hours last night. It was pretty funny, actually."

"Must be nice to be having so much fun," I mutter. "I can't remember the last time I laughed." I realize I haven't heard Dad tell a stupid joke for days either, at least not around me. Meanwhile, Winnie's laughing her head off. "So, is Winnie just naturally happy and carefree? Or is there something about our burned-out barn that brings on her fits of happiness?"

Dakota doesn't answer right away. Then she says, "Hank, if you spent two minutes with Winnie, you'd see how far off you are. Happy? No way. She's got a sadness that runs so deep in her I can feel it."

I stop hammering. "Winnie? Sad? I don't think so. What's she got to be sad about? She gets to go home after all of this. She'll take her horse to her nice barn. And in a few months, she'll be off to OSU to become star of their veterinarian school."

Dakota shakes her head. "She'll be off to a two-year community college. No, I take that back. She won't be 'off' at all. She has to live at home, muck somebody else's stables, and go to school on the side."

"I don't know where you got that," I tell her. "Catman said he and Winnie are going to Ohio State in the fall. Winnie's going into a pre-vet program."

"Not anymore. She doesn't have the money."

I'm still not buying it. "Look, I don't know Winnie that well, but I guarantee she'll find a way to be a vet. It's all she's ever dreamed of."

"Which makes it even sadder. She's given up her dream."

I set down the hammer and try to remember the last time Winnie and I e-mailed about anything except my emergency horse questions. Catman and I haven't stayed in touch either, especially since he took off to film his cat movie. I know there's never been much money in Winnie's family. But surely they could find a way if she really wanted to go to OSU.

"You sure about this?" I ask Dakota.

"Haven't you seen it on her face, Hank?"

Have I? I blew up at her the night they got here. Since then, she's done everything she could to avoid me. And I haven't gone out of my way to be around her either. But when I have seen her, she hasn't looked happy. Dakota's right about that.

Man, the last thing I want to do is feel sorry for Winnie. It was easier being angry.

Dakota picks up a metal bucket and loops the handle over her arm. "I need to go. I told Winnie I'd meet her in the pasture."

"Now? You're leaving *now*?" I want to tack up guidelines, but I can't do it alone.

"I told Winnie I'd–"

"Fine. Forget it," I tell her. "Just go." I bang the nail deeper into the board and try not to let any other sound or thought into my head.

For an hour I do what I can by myself. Then Dad and Uncle Bart get back from Nice.

"Good news, Hank!" Dad says.

"I could use some," I admit.

"The guys at the firehouse got together and volunteered to help us raise the barn on Thanksgiving Day," Uncle Bart answers. "Your dad has some mighty fine friends, if you ask—"

"Thanksgiving? You mean Thursday? This Thursday?" I can't believe Dad thinks we could be ready by then. "That's too soon! Tell them to give us more time."

"No can do," Dad answers. "It's the only day we all have off. Les and Rudy will be on call, but nobody has to go into the firehouse. It's all arranged." There's not a bit of worry in his voice. "We'll be just fine, Son."

But we won't be fine. There's too much to do. I love my dad. I love my uncle. But sometimes it feels like I'm the only man of the house, the only adult. "Dad, think about it. We have to have the frame completely finished before we can raise the barn. That's how it works. There's just not enough time."

"Nonsense," Dad says.

"Nonsense indeed," Uncle Bart agrees.

They work the rest of the afternoon with me. We lay out pieces of the frame. When Mom gets home from the hospital, she trades places with Dad so he can help Aunt Claire get dinner. Uncle Bart lets Mom use his nail gun, and she moves around the frame faster than Uncle Bart and I do.

"Bart, you should at least loosen your tie," Mom insists.

Uncle Bart fingers his Tweety Bird tie like he's afraid she'll try to take it from him. "Say, I'm just fine, Annie, thank you very much."

The sun has already set when Dad calls us in for supper.

"I say we call it a night," Uncle Bart declares. "You know what they say about all work and no play." He helps Mom up, and they start for the house.

I ache all over, but I'm not ready to quit. "Let me finish this corner and I'll be right in."

I stay out until it gets so dark I'm having trouble telling if the boards are square or not. When I turn to go, I almost trip over Kat. "How long have you been sitting there, Kat?"

She shrugs.

"What are you doing out here?"

"Reading," she says. "By moonlight. Are you okay, Hank?"

"I'm fine. Why?"

"Maybe because you're still working. So is Winnie. She's still trying to help that horse.

Everybody else has eaten except you two." When I don't comment, Kat adds, "I've been worried about you."

Kat's the one we worry about. She's the one with cancer. I know better than to say that to her though.

She gets up and points at something behind us. "Don't you think that maple is the most beautiful tree on earth? Has it ever been this red before or held on to its leaves this long?"

I squint at the tree, but it's hard to make out the colors in moonlight. I pick up the hammers, hoping she'll get the hint that I don't have time to chat all day like Catman does. "I really didn't notice the maple today."

"That's what worries me. You used to notice everything."

I stop what I'm doing. She's right. I remember other autumns when the sight of that maple tree shocked me with joy. I'd look at it every day to see the new artwork, God's artwork.

"They're leaving this weekend," Kat says. "You should talk to Winnie before it's too late."

"Why?"

"Because she hasn't noticed the maple

either." Kat walks away, disappearing in moon shadows.

Winnie again. I've thought about talking to her ever since Dakota told me about Winnie giving up her plans to become a vet. I'm not proud of the fact that I've been so hard on her since she got here. She thought she was coming to help our horses. Just because it isn't working out that way doesn't mean I shouldn't be grateful that she's trying. Besides, if Winnie really is as torn up as Kat and Dakota think she is, then I've probably made things worse. I guess it wouldn't hurt me to apologize for getting off on the wrong foot.

Under my breath, I mutter, "You win, Kat." Then I head to the old McCray farm to find Winnie.

By the time I reach the McCray property, a football field's distance from Cleo's pasture, my eyes have fully adjusted to the moonlight. I haven't been out here for a couple of days. The tip of the pasture has been boarded off, separating it into a makeshift round pen. It's a good idea, and for the first time I wonder if Dakota might be right. Maybe Winnie's made more progress with Cleopatra than I figured.

From deep in the pasture, a squeal splits the quiet of the night. The terror in the cry flashes me back to the fire. I can almost hear Cleo screaming from her burning stall.

Then it comes again. This time it's a high-pitched whinny filled with fear. Or anger. Or pain.

There's another cry. The sound is completely different, like it's coming from a different horse, not from Cleo at all. But that can't be. Cleopatra's alone in that pasture.

I take off running the rest of the way, terrified of what I'll find.

The first thing I see is Winnie. She's leaning over the fence, staring into the pasture.

I start to yell for her, but then I see Cleo. The mare is galloping hard, ears back, tail high. She's running from something.

And then I see why. Behind Cleo, chasing that poor mare full speed in the dark pasture, is the white horse. Winnie's horse.

SEVENTEEN

Winnie Willis
Nice, Illinois

I'M SO INTENT ON WATCHING Nickers and Cleopatra that I don't notice anything else until I hear a shout, a human cry invading the night and drowning out the horse squeals. I wheel around and see somebody running out of the bushes like he's on fire.

I freeze. My heart pounds. It's pitch-dark, and I'm alone, a mile from the Rescue.

A gangly figure is racing down the hill, arms flailing. Finally I recognize him. It's Hank.

He keeps coming. Midway down the hill, his foot slips, sending him sliding the rest of the way like he's on a sled. He rolls over and over and lands a few feet away.

"Hank, are you all right?" I reach to help him up, but he pulls his arm away. Fine. He can take care of himself. I get it.

"Why would you put your horse in with Cleo?" Hank demands, kicking clumps of mud from his boots.

"Keep your voice down, will you?" I realize too late that I'm not keeping *my* voice down. Cleo and Nickers are staring at us, taking in the added commotion.

"Look—" Hank starts to shout, then tries again, a couple of decibels lower. "Look, Winnie. I don't get it. Can't you see what your horse is doing to Cleo? Cleopatra doesn't need this. You don't have any idea what that horse has been through."

"Of course I do. That's why I put Nickers in with her. Cleo and I are becoming friends, but it's not happening as fast as I hoped it would. I figured out that what she needs even more than human friendship right now is a horse friend."

"You call this friendship? Look at them!"

Nickers has her ears back and teeth bared.

158

She forces Cleo to back away so fast that the horse rams into the fence.

"Okay," I admit. "They haven't exactly hit it off as buddies. But once Nickers establishes herself as the dominant mare, then Cleo will know she's safe. She'll feel like she's in a herd. She'll understand the pecking order. That's safety to a horse. I think she needs to know where she stands with another horse. And it should give her confidence with people, too."

I don't think Hank's listening to a word I say. He's too into watching the Nickers and Cleo show out in the pasture.

"I know you're trying to help, Winnie. And I appreciate it. We all do. But this isn't working. If I'd known you were planning to do this—"

"Well, you wouldn't know, would you?" I interrupt. "Because you're never out here. You have no idea what's going on with this horse."

"So," Hank says, like he's a volcano trying not to erupt, "that makes two of us then." He turns and storms up the hill, back the way he came.

I stay there and keep an eye on Nickers and Cleo until they're done fighting for position. Eventually they go to separate corners of the pasture, like boxers resting up for the next bout.

✲ ✲ ✲

"How did it go?" Dakota rushes up to me as soon as I walk in the house. It's clear that everybody else has gone to bed.

"I don't know," I answer honestly. "They fought. And Hank was there."

"Hank? So that would explain why he ran in here all mud-covered and mad." Dakota grins at me. "Come on. I made you a sandwich. You can eat it in my room and tell me everything. I want details."

We go to Dakota's room, and I plop onto her hooked rug and scarf down the sandwich. "Hank came running out of the dark and scared me half to death."

"What did he say?"

"Before or after he ordered me to get my wild horse out of there?"

Dakota plops onto the rug with me. "That bad?"

"Worse. Nickers *was* pretty tough on

Cleo," I admit. "She chased Cleo all around the pasture. You should have heard the squeals coming from that mare." I shiver, thinking about it. "Hank did."

"He heard Cleo cry out like that?" Dakota asks. "No wonder he came running. I've never heard squeals like the ones from Cleo during the fire. It was horrible. Hank heard those too. He had to be remembering that."

I hadn't thought about that. I was too busy being defensive. "I don't know. I really thought putting Nickers in with Cleo would be such a good idea. That mare needs the stability horses only get in herds. I knew it might be rough until they had the pecking order worked out. I just didn't know it would be *that* rough."

Dakota scoots over to her dresser and returns with a candy bar. She hands it to me.

"Thanks." I take a huge bite of the chocolate bar. "Maybe I made a mistake putting Nickers in the pasture with Cleo. What if Hank's right? What if I've only made things worse for that poor horse?" I choke on the last word or the candy. "I'm starting to think I shouldn't have come here at all." I shut up because I think I'll cry if I admit anything else.

Dakota scoots closer. She's sitting cross-legged on the rug, facing me. "Winnie, have you prayed about all this stuff?"

"Of course." And it's true. I've prayed for Cleo every day we've been here and even before that.

"I mean," Dakota presses, "have you prayed for yourself? Talked to God about everything–Cleo, Nickers, Hank . . . you. Have you talked to God about veterinarian school?"

I smile patiently at her. "Yeah. I've prayed about it, okay?"

"And?" She's so intense.

"And . . . and if you want to know the truth, praying hasn't made me feel any better. Okay? But I keep praying anyway."

"But doesn't that help?" she asks. "Even if you don't feel it, even if you don't get everything you want, everything you pray for, doesn't it make you feel better to know God's listening? That He loves you so much that He takes time out to hear you?"

I shrug. I want to be excited with her. Her faith is so new. But I'm too tired to fake it.

Dakota sighs. She leans against the bed,

frowning. "Man, I hope that never happens to me."

"What never happens to you?"

"Right now, for me, prayer is totally to this Father who loves me no matter how much I mess up. And believe me, that's not like any father I had growing up." Dakota seems to be struggling with the words, as if she's had a dream and doesn't know how to translate what went on in her dream. She tries again. "When I pray, it feels like God's right in the room with me, you know? Like I'm sitting on God's lap, asking questions and spilling out my guts. Like He's reaching down to love me." She's quiet a minute, and her cheeks turn bright red. "Sounds pretty stupid saying it out loud."

"No, it doesn't," I say in almost a whisper. Because I remember. I remember feeling exactly like that, as if God's love moved with me so close and fresh that all I had to do was think about it and it blew me away. It almost hurts to remember how it used to be.

"I just don't want to lose that kind of a relationship," Dakota says, more to herself than to me, I think. "That kind of love."

Dakota leaves me alone so I can take a bath and get ready for bed. I take a long time. My mind replays what Dakota said about God and love.

After my bath, I'm not sleepy at all. I'm afraid I'll wake Kat if I try to go to sleep in her room. Everybody else is asleep, so I ease downstairs. I'd give anything to be able to talk to Lizzy right now. Dad's called twice since I've been here, but I wasn't in the house. I can't call them back because it's long distance. And I'm the only person on the planet who doesn't own a cell phone.

A dim glow filters into the kitchen and dining room as the computer's screen saver shuffles photos.

If I can't talk to Lizzy, at least I can e-mail her. I log on to my e-mail and see four messages from Lizzy. I scan the first two, all about how she and Barker are loving the Pet Helpline. It makes me miss her even more. And looking at a computer screen isn't the same as having the real Lizzy to talk to.

On a hunch, I decide to check her instant message. Lizzy is online!

WinnieTheHorseGentler: Lizzy! I can't believe you're here.

Lizzy: I couldn't sleep. Must have been God, huh? How are you?

Lizzy: Winnie???

Lizzy: What is it?

WinnieTheHorseGentler: I want to come home. I never should have come here. I'm not helping at all. All I can do is fight with Hank. And I haven't gotten anywhere with Cleopatra. I've probably made her worse. I've barely had time to talk to Kat, and I haven't even helped look for her lost kitten. Plus, Dakota's going to start wishing she had never become a Christian because she's afraid she's going to end up like me. I want to come home! We need the money I'm not making. And I'm worried about Dad and the electric bill and everything there. Oh, Lizzy, what am I going to do?

Lizzy: God loves you, Winnie.

WinnieTheHorseGentler: That's it? That's your answer? I do know that. What I need to know now, though, is—

Lizzy: God loves you so much!

WinnieTheHorseGentler: I know already!

Lizzy: Do you? Because I've been wondering if maybe you forgot.

EIGHTEEN

Hank Coolidge
Nice, Illinois

"HANK!" Kat calls the minute my foot hits the stairs.

"Morning," I call down, amazed that she's up and dressed already. I finish coming downstairs and see that Kat's not alone. Catman's at the counter finishing off a tall glass of orange juice. He's wearing sandals, bell-bottoms, and a tie-dyed shirt. Nobody's going to mistake my hippie cousin for a farmer.

"Guess where we're going!" Kat shouts. She smiles at Catman. "Do you want to tell him, or should I?" she asks him.

"Do your thing, Kat Woman," he says.

"We're going to find my cat!" Kat announces. "And maybe even film her!"

I stare from one to the other. "I don't get it." Maybe they're going to the shelter to get a cat.

"Kitten!" Kat exclaims. "Today we're going to find her. It's taken a while to put all the pieces together, but Catman's got it all figured out."

"Figured out? Figured what out?" My cousin better not be doing what I think he's doing. Not to Kat. "It's great that you're still trying to find Kitten. Just don't get your hopes up."

Her smile fades fast, like somebody dimmed a switch inside her.

Catman takes her hand. "Let's split, my little Kat. Hank forgot. Hopes are meant to be up."

Dakota comes downstairs as soon as Catman and Kat leave. "Where are they going so early?" She yawns and shoves her hair off her face.

"To bring home Kat's kitten, of course," I answer sarcastically. But my sarcasm is weak

168

compared to Dakota's. I don't think she picks up on it.

"Sweet!" she exclaims. "Kat sure has missed that cat of hers."

"You don't really believe they're going to come back with that cat after all this time, do you?"

"Why not?" She walks to the fridge and pours herself a glass of milk.

I follow her. "Why not? Because the cat's been missing so long? Because it was probably in the barn when it burned down? Because Catman's not magic? Kat shouldn't believe everything he says."

Dakota frowns at me. She has a milk mustache. "Kat's prayed for Kitten since she went missing. She believes she'll find her cat. She's not believing in Catman. She's believing in God."

"That's fine," I snap. "That's just great." I'm not sure why I'm so angry, why I'm taking it out on Dakota. "It's all terrific . . . until she hits reality. Until the barn burns or the horse goes crazy or the cat's gone for good!"

Dakota keeps staring, like she can see through me. "Reality? Why would Kat have to hit reality? She's already in it with God, right?

I mean, isn't God smack in the middle of reality?" She takes another swig of milk. "You've known God a lot longer than I have, so maybe I'm missing something here. But I know Kat. She's in this with God, so she'll be okay, no matter what. Hope's a good thing."

Dakota is so new in her faith, so out-there in her trust of God. Was I ever like that? "I'm just saying things aren't always that easy."

"You know, you sound a lot like Winnie," she says.

"Winnie? No way."

"Way," she insists. "Have you heard her talk about giving up hope of becoming a vet?"

When I don't say anything, I feel her gaze on the back of my neck.

"Have you seen her this morning?" Dakota asks.

"Who? Winnie?"

"No. Eleanor Roosevelt," she answers.

I grab my jacket from the coatrack. "She's probably still asleep."

"Are you kidding? She got up a couple of hours ago. Felt like the middle of the night." Dakota yawns again. "I'll bet she's with Nickers and Cleo."

"Did you go along with that move?" I ask her.

"Winnie thought Cleo needed a horse friend. Made sense to me."

"Well, it didn't work. Cleo doesn't need one more worry. I'm going to move the Arabian back to the paddock and give Cleo some peace."

"Hank, that's not a good idea."

The porch door slams behind me as I take off for the pasture.

I glance at the barn, and I'm surprised to see Uncle Bart and Aunt Claire hammering on the frame. "I'll be right back!" I holler at them.

"No hurry!" Aunt Claire hollers back.

I do hurry. But when I come over the last rise in the field before McCrays', I see something amazing, so amazing I have to stop where I am and watch. Cleopatra is standing still a few feet from Winnie and Nickers. The blocked-off tip of the pasture looks more like a round pen now. Winnie's filled in the spaces with an old gate, a ladder, and tree limbs.

Winnie and Nickers are in the center of the makeshift pen with Cleo on the outside. I watch as Winnie steps closer to Cleo, turns, and drops her shoulder slightly. I know enough about training in the round pen to tell that Cleopatra isn't responding all the way yet. She's not running away, but Winnie's giving her the cue to turn and face her. Winnie wants to be given the respect of a dominant partner.

"Not ready yet, Cleo?" Winnie says. "Okay. Your choice, girl. Face me or run. Get it? Back to running." Winnie sends the horse cantering in a circle, still inside the pen.

It's a good system of training a horse, and I've never seen it done as well as I'm seeing it right now. For Cleo, there's no threat of punishment, unless you call making yourself run punishment. The decision to give Winnie the nod as leader is up to Cleo.

The third time around, Cleo slows to a walk. Her lips are moving as if she's chewing gum. Her ears flick up and back. She's definitely paying attention. Then she stops again.

"Good girl, Cleo," Winnie says softly. Amazingly her own horse is still standing statue-still in the center of the blocked-off area. "Now, give me a look, will you?"

Cleo cranes her neck around to give Winnie a good, long look. "Yes. That's it," she says, stepping in closer. Cleopatra doesn't run off. She doesn't look nervous or wary.

I hear Winnie's quiet chatter, but I can't make out the words. It doesn't matter. She steps closer, right up to Cleo's shoulder. Then she reaches up and scratches her neck. Winnie's hand moves skillfully to Cleo's withers, then traces the line of the back all the way to the rump. I know she's getting a good look at the burn. I'm glad for that.

This time when Winnie walks to the center, Cleopatra follows her. Winnie doesn't look back. She doesn't have to. She's the leader, and Cleo's grateful to be led. Winnie the Horse Gentler has gotten through to Cleopatra. I wouldn't have believed it if I hadn't seen it for myself.

The thought hits me hard. *I wouldn't have believed it if I hadn't seen it for myself.*

What's the matter with me? When did Hank Coolidge become someone who wouldn't believe without seeing?

NINETEEN

I TURN FROM THE SCENE of Winnie and the horses, then jog back the way I came.

When I catch sight of the barn, I slow down. I need to think. Too much is happening all at the same time. I need to organize my thoughts, collect them, study them, put them in place again.

"Hank! Hank!" someone hollers across the lawn.

I turn to see Kat running awkwardly toward me with Catman right behind her. She's holding something in her cupped hands.

When she gets closer, I can see the dirty white fur, the scroungy body. *Kitten.*

Kat's panting so hard that I can't tell if she's laughing or crying, if her cat is alive or dead. "Hank, look!" she shouts, walking the rest of the way to me. "We found her!" She holds out her hands, and I see the cat, scrawny and dirty, but definitely alive.

"Kat, that's . . . that's amazing. Where on earth was she?" I stare at the cat, then take in the pure joy on Kat's face.

"She was right by the pond in the south pasture. We think she's been there all along since the fire. She made a hole in this prickly bush on the edge of the pond. I think she liked being near Starlight. She always did like your horse best. That was one of the things Catman picked up on when we talked about Kitten. Plus, I told him how Kitten never acted afraid of water like the other cats. Remember how she used to try to get into the bathtub? Or even in Starlight's water trough! And she always comes to investigate when she hears water running in the sink."

I nod and stroke the cat with my finger.

"Catman thought Kitten might have been

born by water. So that made it her safe place. We were going to look in the old McCray pasture. But then Catman remembered that I'd told him how much Kitten loves Starlight. So we tried the south pasture first. I called and called for Kitten, but she didn't come. We kept searching. And there she was, deep in that bramble bush."

"Is she okay?" I ask, trying to take it all in. "She looks okay."

"Kitten is groovy," Catman says. "Her tail's a little singed. Gives her character."

"She's purring!" Kat exclaims. She clutches her cat and rubs her cheek against the scraggly fur.

"Kat, it's a miracle. I just can't believe—" I stop myself. I'm tired of admitting that I can't believe. I rephrase. "I can't get over it."

"Sure you can, man," Catman says, slapping me on the back before moving off with Kat. "Build a bridge. You can get over it."

＊ ＊ ＊

The rest of the day everybody works together on the barn frame, even Catman. Turns out he's a whiz at carpentry. Kat's cats trail him as he moves around the work area. Winnie and Dakota work side by side refinishing an old desk Gram brought over for the new barn office. Kat makes sandwiches for everybody and walks Wes's dogs so he can help carry lumber.

"Sa-a-ay!" Uncle Bart exclaims above the sawing and hammering. "Why did the turkey cross the road to work at Smart Bart's Used Cars?"

"I don't know, dear," Aunt Claire says.

"Because," Uncle Bart booms, "it was the chicken's day off!"

"Good one, Mr. Coolidge," Aunt Claire says.

I know Dad can't let it go. Even when I was a little kid, I understood the joke wars would go on every time Dad and Uncle Bart got together, especially at Thanksgiving.

Thanksgiving. I'd just about forgotten that tomorrow is Thanksgiving. How could I do that? If Uncle Bart hadn't pulled out a turkey joke, I might have forgotten Thanksgiving until I saw the turkey on the table.

"Why did the police arrest the Thanksgiving turkey?" Dad asks.

Kat, still holding Kitten, takes time to back Dad up. "I don't know. Why did the police arrest the turkey?"

Before Dad can give the punch line, Uncle Bart hollers, "They suspected it of fowl play! Get it? *Foul* play, *fowl* play?"

Dad doesn't laugh. He glares at his brother for ruining his joke. Then he tries again. "What do you get when you cross a turkey with an octopus?" This time he rushes the answer before *somebody* beats him to it. "Lots of Thanksgiving drumsticks!"

"I've got one," Wes announces.

We're silent. Dakota shoots Dad a raised-eyebrow glance. Telling jokes isn't exactly up Wes's alley, but lately he's surprised us with a couple. And they haven't been that bad.

"Go for it, Wes," Dakota urges, "even though the joke competition is really tough around here."

Winnie laughs. She and I are working on opposite ends of the platform floor.

"Okay," Wes begins. "What do you call the feathers on a turkey's wing?"

Nobody ventures a guess.

"Turkey feathers," he answers.

Dakota and Winnie crack up. They laugh on and off for the next few minutes.

"Enough of barn work," Dad says, getting off his knees. "Carry on! I have a couple of turkeys to prepare for tomorrow."

"How many people are we feeding tomorrow?" Dakota asks when Dad's gone.

"Hard to tell," Mom answers. "But they'll all be hungry. Ben and Roger are bringing their whole families."

I didn't realize we were feeding the whole crew. I like Dad's buddies, but I've seen them eat. Meals are social events—long social events. "Mom, they know they're coming to work on the barn though, right? We only have tomorrow to get the barn frame up."

Mom sighs. "Even firemen have to eat, Hank."

We all settle back into the rhythm of work. Nothing but the sounds of sawing, scraping, and hammering can be heard for several minutes.

I try to figure out how much of the work we have to get done before the barn raising. We have two more sections of the frame to build once we get done with the ones we're working on now. We've been at it night and day, but we still have a long way to go. And we're running out of time.

✵ ✵ ✵

After dinner, we all go back to work on the barn. Dad and I are the last two still working several hours after the sun went down. Finally Dad lays down his hammer and rubs his back. "Well, we've made a lot of progress today. We should be fine. We can finish in the morning before the guys come. I think we could all use a good night's sleep." He groans as he gets up off his knees and brushes sawdust from his pants.

When I don't stop hammering, he comes over and puts his hand on my shoulder. "Hank, we're doing all we can. God will do the rest."

I know he wants to say more. He wants *me* to say more. "Go on. I'll be right in."

He sighs, then heads toward the light of the house.

When I finally give in to exhaustion, I head inside and go to bed. The lights are out downstairs except for the night-light over the sink. Plates and silverware are stacked on the dining table, along with bowls and dishes we see only on Thanksgiving and Christmas. The dog-and-cat tablecloth has been replaced by a turkey tablecloth.

I get cleaned up and fall into bed, but I can't sleep. My windows are open. The air is cool enough, but there's no breeze. The night is storm-still, with no sounds filtering in from restless birds or other creatures. Then I hear a low rumble in the distance.

A storm's coming. The next rumble rattles my windows and gets louder and longer. We're in for a big one, and it's moving in fast. If I'd been paying better attention when I was outside, I could have sensed the storm on its way.

And then what? I couldn't have done anything about it. Starlight and the rescues in the south pasture at least have the shelter to stand in if it gets bad. Cleopatra and Blackfire have nothing to protect them from the storm. Neither does Nickers.

TWENTY

A BURST OF THUNDER shakes the whole house. I can't just lie here and do nothing. I pull on my boots and hurry downstairs. The wind has kicked up, howling through the cracks of the house.

When I step outside, I'm pelted with a barrage of leaves. The temperature's dropped, and the wind feels edged with ice. Tree branches crack and groan. Behind the screen door, Wes's dogs bark to get out, then change their minds and quiet down again. The moon and stars have disappeared, as if they're scared of what's coming.

I take off jogging to the south pasture. I have to make sure my horse is all right. I've brought along a flashlight, and I shine the beam in front of me. The path is covered with limbs and debris. When I reach Starlight's pasture, I wave the flashlight back and forth, but the beam's too weak to see anything. The batteries are low.

"Starlight?" I call. I climb over the fence and turn off the flashlight, letting my eyes adjust to the tiny bit of moonlight peeking through the clouds. "Starlight?"

My horse comes trotting from the lean-to. She trots straight to me, as at home in the dark as she is in the light—one of the few benefits of blindness. She snorts and prances, excited by the chilly, electrically charged air and the scent of the storm.

"Good girl," I tell her, scratching her high on the withers. She follows me to the lean-to. Blackfire is huddled to one side, with the two rescued horses gathered at the other end.

I feel a splat on my head, then another big drop of rain on my arm. In an instant, the sky opens fire, shooting pellets of rain. Starlight and I squeeze into the lean-to. Rain and sleet pelt the corrugated roof, crashing and banging against metal. Blackfire whinnies and paws the ground. I try to calm him, but he's pretty much a one-woman horse. I know Dakota must be sleeping through the storm, or she'd be right here with her horse.

I put my arm around Starlight's neck and press my cheek to hers. She's damp, and the smell makes me think of rides we've had in the mist or gentle rains.

How long has it been since I've ridden my horse? I've barely seen her since the fire. "Sorry, Starlight," I mutter. "I love you, girl." She probably hasn't felt my love since the fire, though. She leans into me and rubs her soft muzzle on my neck. "I love you, even though you haven't felt it," I tell her.

The thought rolls around in my head. *Love.* I don't think I've felt God's love since the fire. And even before that. I know enough, believe enough, to realize that God's love for me hasn't changed any more than mine has for Starlight. But it feels like it has.

"I need to check on Cleo," I tell Starlight. "You take care of these guys." I give her a final hug, then dash out of the shelter and into the torrential downpour. In seconds the icy water has soaked me through to the bones.

My boots slosh through puddles and mud as I tread across pastures and fields, heading toward the old McCray pasture and Cleo. The rain slants into my face. I have to shut my eyes partway or I can't see. When I get close, I hear a whinny, then another. Nickers is still in the pasture with Cleo. At least they're together.

I reach the pasture and see that the horses aren't alone. Winnie has both of them on lead ropes. It looks like she's trying to get them to head to the gate.

"Winnie!" I holler. Thunder booms at the same instant I shout.

Winnie looks to the sky, then keeps struggling with the horses.

I run toward her. She wheels around, startled. "What are you doing?" I scream above the wind.

"What are *you* doing?" she screams back.

Cleo gets nervous when I get too close.

"Easy, Cleo," Winnie mutters. The horse calms and quits pulling against the rope. "I want to move both horses to the paddock, where Nickers was before. That okay with you?"

It's a good idea. I don't like Cleo being this far out. And Nickers is good for her. I want to keep them together. "Yeah. Good." I swipe at the water trickling down my face.

"You take Cleopatra!" Winnie shouts.

"No way," I answer. I know I'll just make things worse for her. "That horse has given up on me."

"Fine!" Winnie snaps. "So you're giving up on her? Is that it? You're just quitting and–"

"Hey! Who are you to tell me *I'm* giving up?" I'm yelling, and it's not just the storm that makes the words come out hard and loud. "That's really funny coming from you!"

"Me? I've been down here every day!" she fires back. "I haven't quit on that horse!"

"Well, you've quit on all other horses then! You didn't even get to vet school before you dropped out. I'd call that giving up!" The words come out with a power of their own, and I can tell they cut deep. I don't even know why I said it. She's not the problem. *I* am. "Winnie, I'm sorry. I didn't mean to–"

"Take her!" she shouts, holding out Cleopatra's lead rope to me.

Cleo paws the ground, splattering Winnie with mud.

I shake my head. "I'm making her nervous. I better not get close."

"That's the problem with you, Hank!" Winnie shouts. "You *need* to get close."

I reach for Cleo, but she backs away.

You need to get close. Winnie's words swirl in the air with the rain and sleet and leaves. They're dancing around me, battling to get in. I haven't been close to anything or anyone since the fire. I've kept God so far away that He's had to send the words swirling in the wind to get my attention.

I reach for Cleo again. She jerks her head away, but I take the rope. "Easy, girl."

"Let's get out of here!" Winnie shouts.

I nod. I want to get the horses to the paddock. I want to get out of this storm. I want to get my head straight. I want to get close. These thoughts are the nearest I've been to prayer in a long time.

I follow Nickers and Winnie, and Cleo follows me. Twice she tries to get ahead of me. But I circle her, and she's fine.

The four of us slip and slide through

pastures until we make it to the paddock. Winnie puts Nickers in first, and I follow with Cleo. We shut the gate, and it starts raining harder. I wouldn't have thought it was possible. Sheets of rain slap me from all sides. I'm shivering with the cold.

But somehow it's okay. God has broken through with words that can calm a storm. *You need to get close.*

TWENTY-ONE

Winnie Willis
Nice, Illinois

"**C**OME INSIDE, **W**INNIE!" Hank shouts as he walks toward the house.

The storm rages around us, and I want to be sure Nickers is settled before I leave her. "Not yet!" I shout back, even though I'm freezing. He says something else that's lost in the wind. But when I glance up, I realize that for the first time since I've come to Nice, Hank is looking me straight in the eyes.

"Go on! I'll be right behind you!" I wave him on.

Finally he runs inside.

Cleo's already sidled next to the shed, using the side of the building for shelter. Nickers and I huddle together in the sheets of rain. She nuzzles me, and I stroke her behind her ears.

I'm beyond cold now, beyond wet. This whole night feels like a dream. When I woke up in the middle of the night, I could almost hear Lizzy's voice in the thunder: "*God loves you, Winnie. . . . I've been wondering if maybe you forgot.*"

That's when I got out of bed and headed for Nickers's pasture. I had to make sure she and Cleo were okay. The whole journey to the pasture before the storm broke, Lizzy's words played in my head. I picked up speed. My feet hit the ground to the tune of those words. My heart beat to them all the way to the pasture. "*God loves you, Winnie.*"

And then Hank showed up. Hank. And his angry words crashed into Lizzy's, somehow mixing with them and making them stronger.

"Hank was right," I whisper into Nickers's wet, fuzzy ear. "I did give up."

When did it happen? When did I give up? My earliest memories are of hanging out with horses and watching my mom bandage forelegs and treat cuts. I've always wanted to be a vet.

So when did I give up on that dream? Was it the same time I forgot "*God loves you, Winnie*"?

I blow gently into Nickers's nostrils. She bobs her head. Water flies from her forelock. I blow again. And then I get her answering blow back.

"Nickers, I still want to be a vet."

The wind howls. Thunder roars.

I gaze up through slanting rain into the sky and beyond. "God!" I shout. "I still want to be a vet!" It feels good to say it, to finally admit it, to let God in again. Rain covers me, washing away every objection—the application, the money, the lack of a scholarship. I'm not sure how any of it will work out. But *God loves me*. And that's the answer.

I kiss Nickers good night and race into the house. I kick off my boots and socks in the porch. Dripping wet, I tiptoe upstairs to Wes's room, where Catman is sleeping. "Catman?" I whisper. Then "Catman!" a little louder.

The door opens, and Wes frowns at me. Rex and Lion try to get out, but Wes shuts the door except for a crack. "It's night," he says.

"Sorry. I have to talk to Catman."

The door closes. I don't know if Wes has gone back to bed or what. I'm about to knock on the door again when it opens.

Catman stands in the doorway, his hair spread out like a blond cobweb. He rubs his eyes with his fists and squints at me. "Hey, Willis."

"Hey, Catman."

He comes out into the hall with me, slides to the floor, and pats the floor next to him. We sit side by side, leaning against the wall, listening to rain pound the roof and branches scrape the house.

"You're wet," he observes.

"And cold," I admit.

He puts his arm around my shoulders. We sit like that for several minutes, not talking. It's one of the things I love about Catman. There's no such thing as an awkward silence with him.

Finally my words start coming, and I let them, not taking time to put them in order, just letting them spill like rain between us. "Lizzy wrote me that God loves me and that's the answer."

He nods. "Heavy."

"And she thought maybe I forgot that."

He nods.

"And I think maybe she's right about that." Again, there's a long silence. "I want to be a vet."

"Right on!" he shouts.

I put my hand over his mouth so he won't wake the whole house. "And I'm going to go to Ohio State because they've got the pre-vet classes."

"All true," he says, like he never doubted it.

I lean into him. He smells like soap and rain. "You knew all along, didn't you?"

"I believed all along."

I hug him, and he hugs me back. And it feels good and right. We just sit there in the hallway, while I tell God how thankful I am. I'm thankful for my horse, my family, my life—I'm going to be a vet!—and my Catman. I'm totally thankful.

Suddenly I remember what day it is. "Happy Thanksgiving, Catman!"

"Right on," he agrees. And he kisses me.

Note to self: Never forget this moment.

TWENTY-TWO

Hank Coolidge
Nice, Illinois

I CAN'T SLEEP. I listen to the rain pounding the roof. Branches scrape the windows like they want in.

I guess I fall asleep because when I open my eyes again, it's morning–barely. I get dressed and head outside. The scent of slow-cooked turkey fills the house.

Outside, it's still dark. A bank of gray clouds shields the horizon. I feel like I'm being drawn outside, but the strings drawing me are pulling at me from every direction. For a minute, I don't know which way to go—the paddock, the south pasture, the barn.

And then I know why I've come outside. The maple tree. Kat's maple tree. I want to see it.

I need to see it.

I jog, then run, to the barn. I duck through the frame, wet and splattered with mud. My feet slip, and I go down. My hand slides through mud at the base of the barn. Something brushes against my fingertips, and I jerk my hand away. I get to my knees, then look where my hand was.

Buried beneath mud and ash is a bright red leaf—a maple leaf. I pull it out and see that it's perfect, without a tear or spot, completely preserved. It survived. While flames leaped above it and everything around it turned black, this leaf held on.

Carefully I brush off the ash. "I'll hold on too," I whisper, fingering the veins of the leaf. "I'll stay close, God."

Suddenly I want more than ever to see that maple. The storm and wind have probably blown off all the leaves by now, and I'll never see it the way Kat did. But I want to see it anyway.

I walk around the posts that form the corner of the new barn. When I make the turn, the sun peeks through the clouds, sending a ray, a spotlight that sets the maple on fire with reds, oranges, and yellows. Light shines through the branches, and a breeze makes the wet leaves wave. It's one of the most beautiful things I've ever seen. And I almost missed it.

"Thank You," I whisper.

"Far out."

I turn toward the paddock and see Catman and Winnie, arm in arm, staring at the maple and the sunrise. They're walking toward me, but I don't think they've seen me yet.

I'm grateful that there's someone to share this maple, this moment, with.

You're so good to me. The thought—the prayer—comes to me as natural and real as the sunrise.

"Far out!" I shout. It feels more like prayer than "Amen" or "Hallelujah." So I shout it again: "Far out!"

Catman hollers back, "Right on, man!"

"Far out!" Winnie agrees.

They join me, and we stand gazing at the maple for I don't know how long, soaking up the glory of the tree, the sunrise, and the Creator, who's closer than all of it.

"Hey, guys!" Dakota calls. When we don't answer, she comes over to us and stares at the maple too. "Wow."

"Yeah," I agree.

"Far out." Winnie and Catman say it at exactly the same instant.

"Almost forgot why I came out here," Dakota says. "Hank, your mom says they called from the firehouse. The guys are on their way. She thought you might need us to help you with something before they get here."

I grin at Dakota, then at Winnie and Catman. They look like they're waiting for their work orders. There are a lot of things I can think of that we could do to get ready for the barn raising.

But there's only one that sounds like the perfect way to begin Thanksgiving. "Let's ride."

In minutes, we're on horseback. Catman doubles up with Winnie on Nickers. Dakota and Blackfire ride next to Starlight and me. I've missed my horse, missed the oneness I feel when we move together. But I know she forgives me for being away from her so long. The day is filled with forgiveness. And hope.

Cool wind whips around me. Catman clings to Winnie. Dakota leans forward and hugs Blackfire's neck. I hug Starlight, inhaling her horsey scent. And together, we gallop toward the sunrise, with the whole world in front of us.

Tips on Finding the Perfect Pet

- Talk with your whole family about owning a pet. Pets require a commitment from every member of the family. Your pet should be around for years—ten, fifteen, twenty, twenty-five, or thirty years, depending on the type of pet. Pets can be expensive, especially if they get sick or need medical care of any kind. Make sure you can afford to give your pet a good life for a long time.

- Think like your future pet. Would you be happy with the lifestyle in your house? Would you spend most of your time alone? Is there room for you in the house? If you're considering buying a horse, what kind of life will the horse have? Will someone be able to spend enough time caring for it?

- Study breeds and characteristics of the animal you're considering. Be prepared to spend time with your pet, bonding and training, caring and loving.

- Remember that there is no such thing as a perfect pet, just as there's no such thing as a perfect owner. Both you and your pet will need to work to develop the best possible relationship you can have and to become lifelong best friends.

Consider Pet Adoption

- Check out animal rescue organizations, like the humane society (www.hsus.org), local shelters, SPCA (www.spca.com), 1-800-Save-A-Pet.com (PO Box 7, Redondo Beach, CA 90277), Pets911.com (great horse adoption tips), and Petfinder.com. Adopting a pet from a shelter will save that pet's life and make room for another animal, who might also find a good home.

- Take your time. Visit the shelters and talk with the animal care handlers. Legitimate shelters will be able to provide you with documentation on the animal's health and medical records. Find out all you can. Ask questions. Who owned the pet before? How many owners were there? Why was the pet given away? Is the pet housebroken? Does it like children?

- Consider adopting an adult pet. People tend to favor "babies," but adopting a fully grown animal may be less risky. What you see is what you get. The personality, size, and manners are there for you to consider.

Rescuing Animals

- It's great that you want to help every animal you meet. I wish everyone felt the same. But remember that safety has to come first. A frightened, abused animal can strike out at any time. If you find an animal that's in trouble, call your local animal shelter. Then try to find the owner.

- The best way to help a lost pet find its home again is to ask around. Ask friends, neighbors, classmates, the newspaper deliverer, and the mail carrier. You might put a "Found Pet" ad in the paper or make flyers with the animal's picture on it. But be sure to report the find to your local shelter because that's where most owners will go for help in finding a lost pet.

- Report animal cruelty to your local animal shelter, to the humane society, or to organizations like Pets911 (www.pets911.com/services/animalcruelty).

AUTHOR TALK

DANDI DALEY MACKALL grew up riding horses, taking her first solo bareback ride when she was three. Her best friends were Sugar, a Pinto; Misty, probably a Morgan; and Towaco, an Appaloosa. Dandi and her husband, Joe; daughters, Jen and Katy; and son, Dan, (when forced) enjoy riding Cheyenne, their Paint. Dandi has written books for all ages, including Little Blessings books, *Degrees of Guilt: Kyra's Story*, *Degrees of Betrayal: Sierra's Story*, *Love Rules*, *Maggie's Story*, and the best-selling series Winnie the Horse Gentler. Her books (about 450 titles) have sold more than 4 million copies. She writes and rides from rural Ohio.

Visit Dandi's Web site at
www.dandibooks.com

Can't get enough of Winnie? Visit her Web site to read more about Winnie and her friends plus all about their horses.

IT'S ALL ON WINNIETHEHORSEGENTLER.COM

There are so many fun and cool things to do on Winnie's Web site; here are just a few:

⭐ PAT'S PETS

Post your favorite photo of your pet and tell us a fun story about them

⭐ ASK WINNIE

Here's your chance to ask Winnie questions about your horse

⭐ MANE ATTRACTION

Meet Dandi and her horse, Cheyenne!

⭐ THE BARNYARD

Here's your chance to share your thoughts with others

⭐ AND MUCH MORE!